A LINGERING EVIL

JEFFREY K. SMITH

Printed in the United States of America
ISBN 978-1-64133-676-5 (sc)
ISBN 978-1-64133-677-2 (e)

Library of Congress Control Number: 2021924402

History | Mystery

2022.01.05

MainSpring Books
5901 W. Century Blvd
Suite 750
Los Angeles, CA, US, 90045

www.mainspringbooks.com

This book is dedicated

to the memory of

Buford Ervin Lolley

—gone but not forgotten.

"History is no more than the portrayal
of crimes and misfortunes."
~Voltaire

"Actus non facit reum nisi mens sit rea."
(The act is not criminal unless the intent is criminal.)
~Legal maxim

"Let the punishment match the offense."
~Marcus Tullius Cicero

"Justice, sir, is the great interest of man on earth."
~Daniel Webster

"If you get stuck in jail,
don't call me until the next morning."
~William Travis Smith

FOREWORD

T HIS BOOK IS THE 17TH NON-FICTION book in my "Bringing History Alive" series. It has long been my belief that fact is often stranger and more compelling than fiction. This narrative, however, is only my third foray into the genre of true crime. My first such publication, *Rendezvous in Dallas: The Assassination of John F. Kennedy*, is just one of more than 1,000 books written about one of the most traumatic events of the 20th century. The subjects of my second true crime book, *The Presidential Assassins: John Wilkes Booth, Charles Julius Guiteau, Leon Frank Czolgosz, and Lee Harvey Oswald*, have also been addressed by other authors.

A Lingering Evil: The Unsolved Murder of Buford Lolley is as equally meaningful to me as the first two books, even though the crime has been presented to an infinitely smaller segment of the population via newspaper articles and radio broadcasts from the 1960s and 1970s.

The stories about the brutal murder and two unsuccessful attempts to convict a seemingly innocent man are clearly remembered by many and yet all but forgotten by a few who hail from L.A.—not Los Angeles, but Lower Alabama. More than a half-century ago during the winter of 1968, when I was not yet eight years old, evil visited Enterprise, Alabama and left behind an indelible stain.

As points of clarification, South Main Street and Highway 84 refer to same road. Walker's Dry Cleaners and the Enterprise Laundry are one and the same. In 1968, my hometown newspaper was called *The Enterprise Ledger*. During much of the 1970s, it was renamed *The Daily Ledger*. In the 21st century, the publication is once again known as *The Enterprise Ledger*.

A considerable portion of this book was derived from the recollections of people who were generous enough to allow me to interview them, often more than once. I refused to document what I judged to be salacious and mostly unfounded rumors and innuendoes. Having obtained permission from those individuals, many real names are cited in this book. Some interviewees, however, requested anonymity in exchange for discussing their memories about particular people and events associated with this case. All requests for confidentiality have been honored. In other cases, I exercised my own discretion about using real names, particularly when an individual offered harsh criticism of another person. Without a doubt, many grudges die slow and hard.

In a series of newspaper articles published by *The Daily Ledger* in March of 1975, two witnesses were identified as Mr. X and Mrs. X. I have used a pseudonym on only one occasion because this particular individual could never be directly tied to the Lolley murder case. When I have italicized non-proper nouns, it is for the purpose of emphasizing key words and phrases that may have influenced the outcome of the murder investigation and subsequent trials.

Since the transcripts from both trials were long ago destroyed and neither the Enterprise Police Department nor the Alabama Bureau of Investigation were able to locate their Lolley cold files, I have attempted to seamlessly interject clarifying sentences into the narrative, particularly in the two chapters devoted to the murder trials. Recreating the chronology of those separate trials, using archived newspaper articles and 44-year-old individual and collective memories, was an interesting but arduous task.

Over the years, particularly with continued population growth, Enterprise has certainly been no Utopia, entirely free of illegal activities. However, as of 2021, the town's crime rate is only 47 percent of the national average. The Crime Index, which measures the number of property and violent crimes committed per 100,000 people, is revealing: the national figure is 4,992.7, the state of Alabama is 4,889.7, and Enterprise is 2335.2.

According to figures published by Project Cold Case and The Disaster Center, between 1965 and 2019, there were 947,521 murders committed in the United States. After those crimes were investigated, 626,427 were cleared, leaving behind 321,094 cold cases. In the state of Alabama during that time period, 12,110 out of 26,003 murderers were arrested and convicted—leaving

13,893 cases unsolved. In Coffee County, where I was born and raised, there were 116 homicides, 77 clearances, and 39 cold cases during that 54-year time frame.

More than a half-century ago, murders in South Alabama were not routine occurrences. Brutal murders, particularly during my childhood, were atrocious anomalies. In 1964, Mr. and Mrs. Ed Morgan were stabbed and slashed to death in their Enterprise home by a convict who escaped from a nearby prison work camp. The perpetrator, Ben Mathis, was captured, tried, found guilty, and sentenced to death. Mathis, however, died on Alabama's death row before his rendezvous with the electric chair.

Buford Lolley's murder, no more tragic than the deaths of Mr. and Mrs. Morgan, was somewhat different. There was no escaped convict to blame, and the murderer was never brought to justice.

Pastor John McCrummen, who was born in Enterprise and raised on Bell Street not far from where Lolley was killed, succinctly explained the ramifications of the horrific crime: "It rocked our boat."

I have no grandiose delusion that this book will solve a nearly 54-year-old murder. However, after learning more about the circumstances surrounding Lolley's death, I believe many readers will reach their own conclusions about who committed this crime.

Although only in elementary school when Lolley was murdered, I was disturbed by the heinous crime. In the many years since the mild-mannered gas station attendant was killed, I have often reflected on his unsolved murder. Living in South Carolina for more than 35 years and returning to Enterprise much less often since the deaths of my parents, I nonetheless think about Buford Lolley's murder whenever I drive under the train trestle on South Main Street and approach the former location of the Save-Way gas station. As I write this, I am reminded that time is fleeting. Now a decade older than Lolley was in January of 1968, if I am going to tell this story, the time is at hand.

In addition to documenting the events surrounding a brutal murder and its prolonged aftermath, it is equally important to remember the life of the victim. Buford Lolley, a decent and hard-working man, was targeted by a savage killer. He did not deserve that fate, and his family should never have been forced to endure the sudden, unexpected grief.

The surviving family members of the late David Hutto, the man who was ultimately acquitted of murdering Lolley, have also suffered. At the very least, they deserve an opportunity to have an unbiased light shined on the man they knew and loved. Therefore, I invite you to take a trip back in time to the place I will forever call home.

Historian William Manchester once wrote that 1968 was "the year everything went wrong." In January, Americans learned they had been lied to by their own government after North Vietnam launched the surprise Tet Offensive. Consequently, it became quite apparent that the combined military forces of the United States and South Vietnam were not going to triumph over the enemy in the foreseeable future, if ever. By the time the final U.S. combat troops withdrew from South Vietnam five years later under the short-lived fallacy of peace without victory, nearly 60,000 American soldiers and support personnel had been killed in a failed effort to prevent the spread of Communism.

In January of 1968 alone, 16,899 American soldiers died in the jungles of Southeast Asia. The growing unpopularity of the Vietnam War ultimately convinced President Lyndon Johnson to announce on March 31st that he would not seek reelection.

Unfortunately, the violent acts committed in 1968 were not limited to distant battlefields. On April 4th, civil rights leader Dr. Martin Luther King was assassinated on the balcony of the Lorraine Motel in Memphis, Tennessee. Then on June 5th, shortly after midnight after addressing supporters who were celebrating his twin victories in the South Dakota and California Democratic presidential primaries, Senator Robert F. Kennedy was gunned down by an assassin at the Ambassador Hotel in Los Angeles. Not yet five years had elapsed since his older brother, President John F. Kennedy, had been assassinated in Dallas, Texas. Despite several hours of emergency neurosurgery, Robert Kennedy failed to regain consciousness and died just over 24 hours after he was shot in the back of the head with a .22 caliber revolver. Like Lee Harvey Oswald before them, King's assassin, James Earl Ray, and Bobby Kennedy's assassin, Sirhan B. Sirhan, forced their infamous names into the annals of American history.

Then, in late August of 1968, violent confrontations erupted in the streets of Chicago. As delegates to the Democratic National Convention were preparing to nominate Hubert Humphrey as the party's presidential candidate, anti-Vietnam War protestors engaged in bloody street fighting against the combined forces of the Chicago Police Department and the Illinois National Guard. Those ugly images were seen by millions of television viewers throughout the country.

Many wondered if the violence in 1968 was ever going to end. It was a most troubling year in what proved to be one of the most tumultuous decades in US history.

For many Americans, Sunday, January 14, 1968, was a time for relaxation. That afternoon, the Green Bay Packers defeated the Oakland Raiders to win Super Bowl II. Alabama's own Bart Starr was named the game's most valuable player after passing for 202 yards and throwing a touchdown pass. Meanwhile, Beatles fans were delighted to learn that *Hello, Goodbye* had simultaneously topped popular record charts in both the United States and the United Kingdom.

In Enterprise, Alabama, January 14th was unseasonably cold. The temperature on this Sunday morning dropped to 24 degrees, and the mercury only climbed 12 degrees before day's end. For those accustomed to living in the Deep South, the frigid weather conditions were particularly harsh. By comparison, in the month of January, the average high in Enterprise was 61 degrees, and the average low was only 37.6 degrees.

For many local residents, the morning was occupied with Sunday school, immediately followed by the regular worship services at their respective churches. Afterward, many surely enjoyed a home-cooked dinner—yes, dinner because evening meals in South Alabama were referred to as supper. In other words, Southerners ate dinner at the same time Yankees consumed lunch. Many adults, particularly those who had to work six days a week, likely indulged in the luxury of an afternoon nap.

While the residents of Enterprise were certainly not without their individual problems, the prospect of a violent crime was very low on their list of concerns. Only in recent years, after Mr. and Mrs. Morgan were murdered, did many even bother to lock their doors before retiring for the evening.

The tranquility of this particular sabbath day was disrupted by rapidly spreading news about an atrocity committed in the wee hours of the morning on the south side of the town's main thoroughfare.

PROLOGUE

The Summer of '67

To better understand the true meaning of evil and injustice, it is helpful to appreciate the root causes of innocence and naivete. When we are young, the concept of self and others is heavily influenced by other people, the environment, and personal experiences. In the summer of 1967, a half-year before Buford Lolley was murdered, at least one boy's capacity for trust had not yet been seriously violated.

Enterprise, Alabama was all that I really knew, and 402 Mixson Street seemed like a pretty good place to live. Our town, like many others in the South, had an audible regularity. Six times a day—at 5:45 a.m., 6:00 a.m., 1:45 p.m., 2:00 p.m., 9:45 p.m., and 10:00 p.m., the steam whistle at the cotton mill loudly announced its presence. You could set your watch by that whistle, knowing it was time to get up in morning, early afternoon hours were nearing their end, and bedtime was close at hand. At a quarter before the hour, a short blast resonated throughout the community, reminding mill laborers that they had 15 minutes before the next work shift started. A longer blast at the top of the hour meant the gates were closed for the next eight hours. Those who failed to make it inside the mill before whistle blew a second time lost a day's pay.

Even if they were not blood kin, people tended to look out for each other. In my eyes, there seemed to be an informal but sophisticated adult spy organization: if you were caught misbehaving at a neighbor's house, the news would be transmitted to one or both of your parents before you returned home and were afforded an unsuccessful opportunity to plead your case, which offered little more than a brief respite from the eventual punishment. While not fully understood or appreciated at the time, in retrospect, this proved to be an effective system for differentiating right from wrong and learning to accept responsibility for your actions.

Having long been taught to be respectful of adults, I also craved their attention. My best friend's mother and father, who lived across the street, readily and lovingly added an honorary fourth son to their family. A half-century later, when I was a middle-aged-man and learned of the deaths of my second set of parents, I unashamedly shed tears.

As a boy, I was gleeful, angry, sad, remorseful, and frustrated, but never bored. In an era long before the internet, cell phones, and video games, there always seemed to be plenty of enjoyable activities to occupy my time after completing my assigned chores. Of equal importance, I did not necessarily need company to experience contentment. With a tennis ball, baseball glove, and one of the brick walls of our house, it was possible to create nine-inning baseball games on an imaginary diamond. I also enjoyed reading, and with a library card and a reliable bicycle, I explored new worlds while developing a lifelong passion for books.

And there were always dogs, a source of unconditional positive regard. My father raised beagles, some to sell as puppies to supplement our family's income and others to track rabbits. In the summer of '67, hunting season was a few months away. Even if rabbit season had officially started, my father never took his dogs out until after the first frost, when the rattlesnakes went into hibernation. A rattler's bite more often than not was fatal to a beagle. I abhorred killing innocent creatures, but since my father rarely shot anything, I tagged along to spend more time with him. We two hunters and our hounds didn't take to the woods for rabbit meat. My father simply enjoyed listening to the barking of the beagles, all of whom he could identify simply by the sound of their excited yelps—Buddy, Sugarfoot, Nellie, and Judy, to name just a few. Most of the time, I merely endured the hunting trips, but never lost my affection for dogs.

Turtle farming could be a solitary or group venture. The creek (my parents called it a branch), running behind our house was filled with terrapins and even a few loggerheads. After being captured with a shovel and a bucket, the smaller hard-shell reptiles spent their summer months vacationing inside a number two washtub, partially filled with water and bricks, which allowed them to periodically bask in the sun. The larger ones, usually loggerheads, were housed in what had once been a large concrete-walled outdoor goldfish tank my father had constructed years ago atop a natural spring.

Balls of bread kneaded from the end pieces of Sunbeam or Colonial loaves augmented with worms and bugs kept the small herd of reptiles well fed with a seemingly balanced diet of carbohydrates and proteins. Around Labor Day and the start of the coming school year, the turtles were returned to their natural habitat, and the washtub was put away until the following summer.

If you could muster enough companions, yard tackle football, absent pads or helmets, was never restricted to the traditional fall season. The rough-and-tumble gridiron competition might occasionally result in cuts, bruises, and hurt feelings but never any documented fractures or concussions.

The construction of dams at a favored spot on the creek, which without much thought or originality, was christened "the deep part," was invariably a group activity. Using shoveled dirt reinforced with tree limbs, my friends and I undertook small engineering projects. After the aquatic barrier formed a reservoir that threatened to overflow the creek bed, the real fun began. If you were lucky enough to obtain a handful of cherry bombs (yes, they were still legal at that time), the designated demolition expert would place them at strategic positions on the recently constructed dam and connect the explosives with a common fuse. The implosion specialist, who also functioned as the fuse lighter, had to have a steady hand and fleet feet to complete the designated assignment before joining his companions, who were clustered a safe distance away. A single cherry bomb was rumored to generate enough force to separate a urinal from the wall of schoolhouse boys' room. Without a doubt, four or five them, igniting within seconds of each other, would obliterate a creek dam.

The wooded area by the creek served as the ideal make-believe battlefield. Self-dug foxholes surrounded by plentiful bramble, brush, and trees along with a well-equipped arsenal of toy carbines, M-16s, and hand grenades, enabled the junior Green Berets to repel any number of imaginary foreign invaders. The frontal assaults and flanking maneuvers of the youthful combatants simulated tactical warfare at its finest.

Just behind our house and immediately adjacent to the creek, the root system of a once-towering hardwood had been compromised by wind and water. The end result of mother nature's handiwork, the so-called "slanting tree," extended upward at a roughly 30-degree angle. With only a slight bit of coordination, you could simply walk up the tree trunk to its topmost branches, where we constructed a platform-only tree house with hammers, nails, and discarded sheets of plywood. Our treetop lair remained functional for years to come.

The chopper game could be a solo test or small-group competition. During the height of the Vietnam War, helicopter overflights in Lower Alabama were as ubiquitous as the summertime mosquitos and redbugs. Without looking skyward, a contest participant had to guess the type of aircraft from the sounds generated by its engine and rotor blades. Was it a Huey, a Cobra, or a Sioux? Sometimes, the aircraft gave itself away—if the pilot of a Chinook tilted the aircraft's twin rotors at a certain angle, the deafening chop rattled windowpanes within a half-block radius.

In retrospect, chasing the "bug truck" was likely our most daring adventure. Once or twice each week, a pick-up truck dispatched by the city government traveled down Mixson Street spraying a smoky stream of insecticide in its wake. It was a rite of passage to mount your bicycle and chase the vehicle, all the while enveloped in a blinding cloud of noxious fumes. It is not known how deadly the gas was to mosquitos but none of the youthful trailers was known to have developed early-onset pulmonary or neurological illnesses.

At least until midday on Saturdays, I helped my father with various chores, such changing the oil in the car or dipping the beagles in 55-gallon drums filled with concentrated liquid flea and tick killer. Every third Saturday, however, the day began with a 50-cent haircut at Shorty's barbershop. There was never very much red hair to be shorn, as my father strictly enforced World War II boot camp buzz-cut standards. Despite his name, Shorty Evans was anything but diminutive in height or trim in body build and seemingly had an endless supply of George C. Wallace campaign literature stacked beside the cash register. Whether or not Shorty ever met Alabama's governor in person, the barber nonetheless was a self-appointed Enterprise-area Wallace campaign coordinator.

I always referred to the acceptance of money from my father as pay day. The word allowance made me feel like I was being rewarded for doing nothing. Despite my other shortcomings, I never wanted to be grouped with the much-maligned welfare recipients. Mowing the lawn, picking up limbs after a thunderstorm, and washing the car were regularly assigned duties, payable at the rate of $2 a week. The wages paid by my father were never adjusted for inflation and ended abruptly when I became a teenager and started my first real job at Hilmac Sporting Goods on North Main Street.

After stuffing a small wad of designated spending cash in the pockets of my cutoff jeans, I commandeered my trusty Sears and Roebuck bicycle, equipped with a banana seat and chopper handlebars, and pedaled up town. The prime places to shop on Main Street included Butner's, a dime store, and Jerry's Toy Store. The latter contained large bins filled to the brim with much-coveted Hot Wheels and Matchbox cars.

If the yearnings of my sweet tooth outweighed the desire to add to an already well-stocked inventory of toy cars, Andrews Sweet Shop whipped up exquisite milkshakes. The ultimate in refreshing beverages, fountain-style Coca-Cola, was available at Bryars–Warren Drug Store. The Big R drive-in restaurant, which offered no interior seating and just a handful of picnic tables covered by an awning adjacent to the railroad track, dispensed spicy root beer in addition to burgers, hotdogs, and fries. If my timing was right, a trip to the Big R featured live entertainment in the form of a passing freight train. With advanced warning from the engineer's horn as the locomotive neared the Damascus Road overpass, it was possible to place a penny, or a nickel if I was feeling unusually wasteful, on the steel rail and await its utter flattening by the wheels of at least one train engine and a dozen or more freight cars. For some strange reason, I considered smashed railway coins to be collectibles and good-luck charms.

Vacations, even long weekends, were a rarity in our house, a byproduct of tight finances and my parents lack of wanderlust. If I wanted to dip my toes in the waters of the Gulf of Mexico and marvel at the waves lapping onto the snow-white beaches, I was dependent on the kindness and generosity of other adult family members or trusted neighbors. While it was only 90 miles from Enterprise to Panama City Beach, Florida, easily a day excursion, my father considered it wasteful and indulgent and derisively referred to seawater as croton oil.

The Levy Theater on East College Street was the ultimate entertainment venue. The admission fee was fixed—35 cents for one movie and 50 cents for a double feature. If so inclined, I could spend an additional quarter at the snack bar and purchase a large Dr. Pepper and a box of Milk Duds. With its always-sticky floors, a larger-than-life movie screen, and 600 seats, the Levy often featured films appealing to my wildest fantasies, including westerns featuring a young Clint Eastwood and James Bond 007 spy thrillers.

Television was always an evening delight, particularly in the summer, when there was no fixed bedtime. A seven-year-old boy, who might be considered precocious today, was then regarded as a nerd, particularly if I inadvertently admitted to my peers something I had seen the night before on NBC's Huntley–Brinkley Report.

The choice of television networks required very little in the way of imagination or effort. Broadcasts from WTVY, Dothan's channel 4 CBS affiliate, and NBC's channel 12, which originated from Montgomery's WSFA studios, were almost always clear and audible. The ABC affiliate—call letters and channel number long since forgotten—was in Columbus, Georgia, but the broadcast signal was too remote for most chimney-mounted aerials to capture. Even with a two-channel limit, the programs were still classics, including *The Andy Griffith Show, Gunsmoke, Bonanza, Wild Kingdom*, and *The Wonderful World of Disney*. A few years later, cable television made its debut in our household, but the unused aerial stayed in place for many months until harsh winds from a thunderstorm ripped it away.

Was I bored? Never. Was I socially awkwardly, innocent, and unworldly? Yes. I had been too young to remember the 1964 murders of Mr. and Mrs. Ed Morgan in Enterprise or the national tragedy when President Kennedy was assassinated on November 22, 1963. The assassinations of Martin Luther King and Robert F. Kennedy, occurring in April and June of 1968, came a few months after the barbaric killing on Enterprise's South Main Street. And perhaps the most demonic of them all, the murderous rampage of the Manson family in California, was still two years away.

After the passage of nearly 54 years, as best as I can remember, my first real encounter with an evil that defied understanding was the murder of Buford Lolley.

CHAPTER 1

Cold, Dark, and Dead

IT WAS NEARLY 1:00 A.M. ON January 14, 1968, before Joe Ray Hudson finally had an opportunity to stretch his legs, having spent a portion of late Saturday night and early Sunday morning sitting with a family member who was dying of cancer. After being relieved by another relative, Joe Ray left the Hildreth Street residence where he had spent the past few hours and discovered the sky was mostly clear, but the temperature was extremely cold. After starting his car, Hudson realized the windshield was covered with a thick coat of frost. Rather than travel all the way home hampered by limited visibility, he opted to make the 0.2-mile drive to the Save-Way gas station at 716 South Main Street and planned to wait there until the defroster melted away the ice. At the same time, he could shoot the breeze with his close friend, Buford Lolley, who worked at the Save-Way.

As Joe Ray eased his automobile under the station's canopy, which extended from the front of the building and provided cover for four regular and premium grade gas pumps, compressed air and water hoses, and two 55-gallon drums used for trash disposal, he immediately recognized the portly man dressed in his customary work attire: well-worn denim overalls. The graveyard shift gas station attendant was sitting in an overstuffed chair positioned against the back wall of the cinder-block building. Hudson stepped out of his car and headed inside, carefully negotiating the six-inch drop from the outside of the station to the building's interior concrete floor. As he neared the front door, Hudson passed a coin-operated Coca-Cola

1

machine and an STP decal affixed to one of two large windows on either side of the station's main entrance. The large gas storage tanks were above ground and positioned to the rear of building, clearly out of his line of vision.

Even though it was below freezing, Lolley kept the station's wooden and glass-paned front door wide open so he could see and hear approaching night-owl customers. In the late 1960s, filling station attendants were not only responsible for pumping gas into your car, but also checking the engine's oil level and washing the windshield. A kerosene-fueled space heater, positioned near the wall to the right of Lolley's chair, kept the temperature inside the 18-foot by 20-foot structure at least bearable, even when the door was not closed.

Fifty-one years old, Lolley had worked the overnight shift for more than a dozen years at the only 24-hour gas station located in Enterprise. In an era before around-the-clock convenience stores were commonplace, at least in small to medium-sized towns in Lower Alabama, Lolley likely sold more cigarettes, candy bars, chewing gum, and condoms than gasoline during the early-morning hours.

Save-Way was an independently operated gas station and was not equipped with garage bays to accommodate car repairs. A raised-letter sign, SAVE WITH SAVE-WAY, stood atop the building. The station's proprietor, Leon Devane, worked more than 12 hours each day while his wife worked at the local dime store. In early 1968, J.P. Strickland covered the evening hours before Lolley provided coverage during the late night and wee hours of the morning.

Devane, an incessant tobacco chewer, customarily wore overalls topped with either a straw hat or a fedora. One local citizen described the gas station owner as "a good guy who dressed like a bum." According to a former bank employee, despite outward experiences, Devane was a savvy and prosperous businessman. In an era of so-called gas wars, when station owners constantly tried to undercut the competition's price per gallon, Devane seemed to hold his own.

"Nobody sold more gas than my daddy," his son, Vance, recalled, "He worked from 4:30 in the morning until 6:00 at night, seven days week."

Even though they were not blood kin, Joe Ray Hudson and Buford Lolley were longtime friends. However, there was a loose family connection: Hudson's wife was the sister of Buford's sister-in-law, Mavis Lolley.

"We were like family," Joe Ray's daughter, Karen Hudson Miller, recalled.

After Hudson arrived that fateful night, the two men made small talk for a few minutes while the sheet of ice on Hudson's windshield melted. They might have started their conversation discussing the weather, as men of a certain age have long been known to do. And whether or not it was mentioned at that time, a .32 caliber pistol was stored in a lockbox on a shelf in the rear of the building.

"Buford, don't put that pistol in the lockbox," Leon Devane had told his affable employee many times over, to no avail.

Hudson and several others had also repeatedly warned Lolley he should keep the weapon is his pocket while working alone during the middle of the night. Trusting by nature, the gas station attendant always calmly disregarded their advice.

"No one's going to bother me if I leave them alone," Buford innocently explained.

After a few minutes, Joe Ray drove home, leaving Lolley by himself once again. Joe Ray would be among the last people to ever talk to Buford.

Before daybreak, Lolley was savagely murdered.

CHAPTER 2

The boll weevil

THE PSYCHOLOGICAL IMPACT OF NEGATIVE EVENTS on an individual's sense of well-being is governed by innate resilience and the adaptiveness of their coping mechanisms. The effect of traumas is also mitigated by a person's past experiences, which is often dictated by one's locale.

To better understand the frequency and severity of traumatic experiences, it is useful to examine one's surrounding environment. While equally tragic, a murder in New York City in 1968 did not mean the death would be covered on the front pages of newspapers unless the victim was a well-known public figure. In a small town, however, homicide was an aberration, one that disrupted the largely tranquil social milieu. Consequently, it's helpful to know more about where Buford Lolley lived and how his murder affected his fellow citizens.

The scene of Lolley's murder, Enterprise, Alabama, has its own unique history. Like other communities, the town has seen it shares of joys, sorrows, and eccentricities.

Located 75.9 miles south–southeast of the capital city of Montgomery, 28 miles north of the Florida border, and 50 miles west of the Georgia state line, Enterprise is part of the so-called tri-state area. The region is also referred to as the Wiregrass, deriving its name from the botanical species *Aristida stricta*, otherwise known as wiregrass. With a texture akin to wire, it is a warm-season flora native to North America and extremely common in the sandhills and coastal plains of the Carolinas and southeastern United States.

Enterprise occupies the southeast portion of Coffee County, whose map shape resembles a rectangle with a much smaller rectangular portion of the upper left corner missing. The county is named in honor of General John Coffee, who fought in the War of 1812 and led battles against the Creek Indians in the 19th century. A portion of the town includes a small chunk of southwest Dale County, the namesake of Samuel Dale, a pioneer who led a group of settlers to southern Alabama.

The area is known for generally mild winters. Anything more than snow flurries is a once-in-a-decade-or-two occurrence. While spring and summer are pleasant, summers can be long and brutal. According to the Köppen climate classification system, Enterprise is classified as "humid and subtropical." Beginning as early as May and extending into September, daily highs can reach into the triple digits, with the humidity readings not far behind.

Over the years, Enterprise has grown steadily. According to census records, Enterprise's population was 26,562 in 2010. A decade later, the number of residents had increased to 28,711—a growth of 7.48 percent. According to the census, Enterprise's ethnic mix was 69.49 percent Caucasian, 22.57 percent African American, and 7.94 percent other races. As of 2020, Enterprise was the 19th largest city in Alabama and the 1,343rd largest city in the United States.

In its early days, Enterprise was predominately an agriculture-based economy. As of 2021, Coffee County was still the top agriculture producer in Alabama and in the top 100 of nearly 3,000 counties nationwide. With the passage of time, Enterprise's economy, on a percentage basis, has become equally divided among agriculture/agribusiness, military, industrial production, retail businesses, and service industries.

The origin of Enterprise dates back to the late 19th century. In 1880, William J. Aberson arrived at a spot in southeast Alabama where two wagon trails crossed and pine trees grew abundantly. John Henry Carmichael, who lived in nearby Haw Ridge on the Dale and Coffee county line, purchased a large parcel of land from Aberson in those same uninhabited piney woods. In 1881, after moving to the site of his newly acquired land holdings, Carmichael, who is credited as the founder of what was destined to become a thriving community, built a house for his family and opened a general store. A year later, the post office, originally established in the settlement of Drake Eye five miles to the north, was relocated to Carmichael's newly constructed home.

By 1896, 250 people had settled in the area, and the city of Enterprise was officially incorporated. The origin of the town's name is believed to come from the meaning of the word itself. According to the Merriam-Webster dictionary, enterprise is defined as "a systematic purposeful activity." Not surprisingly, John Henry Carmichael was elected as the town's first mayor.

Carmichael liberally divided his significant property holdings, selling lots to new settlers. He also donated land for construction of a Methodist church and the town's first cemetery. When a federal land grant office opened in 1897, the agency was charged with selling an additional 3,560 acres. When John Henry Carmichael died in 1898, he held the distinction of having served as Enterprise's first merchant, postmaster, and mayor.

The Alabama Midland Railroad eventually extended its tracks to Enterprise, with the first passenger train arriving on February 14, 1898. A number of those who journeyed to the area decided to call Enterprise home. Within 10 years of its incorporation, the town's population had grown to 3,750 residents. The citizens proudly erected a banner across Main Street: "Pull For Enterprise or Pull Out."

By 1903, the locals determined Enterprise needed a "transportation focus." Consequently, the first train depot was constructed. That same year, the Rawls Hotel opened on Main Street adjacent to the depot, and both sites became prominent destinations for social mingling.

In the early 20th century, cotton was the predominate cash crop in Enterprise and the surrounding area. Cultivation of cotton, however, was a risky proposition. *Anthonomus grandis*, commonly known as the boll weevil, soon made its destructive presence known in southeastern Alabama. A beetle with only a three-week life span, the boll weevil ravenously feeds on cotton buds and flowers. Thought to be native to Central America, the pest had migrated to the United States from Mexico in the late 19th century.

After 60 percent of the 1915 cotton crop in the Enterprise area was decimated by a boll weevil infestation, local farmers were at a loss. Enterprise banker H.M. Sessions and county extension agent John Pittman worked in conjunction with George Washington Carver, an African American agronomist, to study and revise agricultural practices in the area.

Born around 1864, Carver was the first black student to attend Iowa State University, where he studied agriculture, earning both undergraduate and master's degrees. In later years, he was awarded an honorary PhD by the university. In 1896, Booker T. Washington, the president of Tuskegee Institute in east central Alabama, invited Carver to join the faculty and head its agricultural department.

Carver was a strong proponent of environmentalism, crop rotation, and halting soil erosion. He also encouraged farmers to diversify cotton production and start growing other crops, including peanuts, sweet potatoes, and soybeans. In one of his 44 practical bulletins for farmers, Carver included 105 recipes for peanuts.

The resulting analysis of the soil and climate in the Enterprise area proved it was the prime location for growing peanuts. Although cotton farming was never fully abandoned, a new cash crop became king.

By 1917, Coffee County was America's largest producer of peanuts. More than a century later, the legume remains an agricultural mainstay. About half of all peanuts grown in the United States are cultivated within a 100-mile radius of Dothan, Alabama, which is just 30 miles east of Enterprise.

Absent the devastation wrought by boll weevils, agricultural practices in Enterprise and the surrounding area might have remained tenuous, and the farm economy might never have prospered. Consequently, Roscoe Owen "Bon" Fleming, an Enterprise businessman and city councilman, came up with the idea of building a monument to honor the boll weevil. At a cost of $1,800, a metal statue was crafted either in Italy or Bama Foundry Company in Montgomery—some believe the story about European construction was concocted for show. Either way, a generous Fleming paid $3,000 out of his own pocket for construction, delivery, and installment of the monument.

As the second decade of the 20th century was nearing its end, Enterprise erected the Boll Weevil Monument in the center of Main Street. Formally dedicated on December 11, 1919, the monument's significance was denoted by a sign that still stands at the southeast corner of Main and College Streets: "In profound appreciation of the Boll Weevil and what it has done as the Herald of Prosperity, this monument was erected by the Citizens of Enterprise, Coffee County, Alabama."

In what was likely a controversial decision in the uncompromising era of racial segregation, Bon Fleming invited George Washington Carver to deliver the main address during the dedication ceremonies. Carver, however, was unable to attend because flooding had washed out sections of the railway lines between Tuskegee and Enterprise.

The monument today features a white-painted metal neoclassical Greek woman dressed in a peplos, a body-length garment commonly worn by women in ancient Greece. Standing a shade over 13 feet tall, she holds an oil lamp aloft with a replica of a boll weevil resting on top. The ornate base, featuring two rounded streetlamps, sits in the center of a fountain that can accommodate running water or greenery and is surrounded by wrought-iron railing. To date, the Boll Weevil Monument is the only statue in the world glorifying an agricultural pest and is recognized as a member of the National Register of Historic Places.

Interestingly, the original monument featured a fountain on top rather than its namesake pest. Eventually, the top fountain spout was shut off because the water pressure kept the surrounding street wet. In 1948, Luther Baker, an area artisan, constructed a boll weevil replica from linotype metal, roughly the size of a man's fist. Baker's creation was placed atop the unused fountain on the oil lamp.

Mischief has plagued the monument over the years. When the surrounding ground-level fountain is operational, it has not been unusual for pranksters to fill the pool with laundry detergent. The resulting boll weevil bubble baths have sometimes occurred on Friday nights when a significant portion of Enterprise's population was attending an out-of-town high school football game.

In the winter of 1953–54, unknown bandits stole the boll weevil, which was never recovered. In short order, the Enterprise Pilot Club assumed responsibility for replacing the purloined pest. Charles Deloach, a reporter for *The Enterprise Ledger,* designed a new boll weevil from plaster of Paris. Afterward, members of the Pilot Club took the model to Montgomery, where it was cast into metal. The new boll weevil was proudly unveiled atop its pedestal on May 1, 1954, accompanied by a celebratory parade, including floats and marching bands.

In 1971, a soldier who was stationed at nearby Fort Rucker and likely quite inebriated, took direct aim at the monument with his car. In the aftermath of the high-speed collision, the length of his automobile was shortened by nearly a foot, the driver apparently emerged unhurt, and the Boll Weevil Monument survived with only a bit of paint chipped from its base.

In early May of 1974, a bolder band of thieves swiped not only the boll weevil but also the rest of the statue. The monument's badly broken centerpiece was eventually discovered near a bridge on Highway 27, the road connecting Enterprise with the neighboring town of Ozark. After several days of intense labor, the historic marker was repaired. On Friday, May 24, 1974, under the auspices of the Pea River Historical Society, the refurbished Boll Weevil Monument was once again unveiled to the public.

In 1981, robbers again made away with boll weevil, which was never returned. The replacement, cast in such a way that it would be more difficult to cut from the pedestal, was erected in July of that same year. Three days later, Roy Shoffner, publisher of *The Enterprise Ledger*, wrote an article entitled: "WELCOME BACK, BOLL WEEVIL MONUMENT."

On July 11, 1998, the boll weevil was stolen yet again. The bandits unceremoniously detached the beloved insect and vandalized the statue, breaking off the grand lady's arms. Having become an irresistible lure for an unusual breed of thieves, or maybe just dedicated pranksters, the boll weevil was replaced with an unbreakable polymer–resin replica, making it more difficult and less tempting to steal.

On December 11, 2019, a ceremony was held commemorating the centennial of the Boll Weevil Monument. On that occasion, a marker honoring Dr. George Washington Carver, H.M. Sessions, John Pittman, and Bon Fleming was unveiled.

On March 1, 2007, Enterprise garnered national attention in an unfortunate way. In the early afternoon, an EF-4 tornado took direct aim at the town. The tornado's three-quarter-mile swath targeted business and residential areas, leaving behind an estimated $307,000,000 in damages. Eight students at Enterprise High School, which was in the direct path of the devastating tornado, were killed when a section of the structure's walls and ceilings collapsed. The high school building, which had opened in 1958, was almost totally demolished, and the adjacent Hillcrest Elementary School was severely damaged.

A ninth person died when the tornado struck her residence. In the end, more than 120 people were injured by the killer storm. Two days after the twister touched down, President George W. Bush visited Enterprise to survey the devastation.

As a result of storm damage and size restraints at the existing location, a new high school was constructed at a much larger site, costing approximately $100,000,000. In the interim period, high school students attended classes at Enterprise State Community College, where trailers were used as portable classrooms. The new high school and its spacious campus opened on August 22, 2010.

The extensive damage wrought by the tornado necessitated construction of a more modern and larger Hillcrest Elementary School at the approximate site of the original structure. In the meantime, students attended classes at another elementary school on a half-day basis and used the newly constructed Enterprise Early Education Center. On August 12, 2009, Hillcrest Elementary School, which had been rebuilt at a cost of $13,000,000, opened its doors to 560 students.

As of 2021, the nearest city to Enterprise with a population of 1,000,000 or more was Houston, Texas. While never destined to become a major metropolitan area, the community has continued to experience significant growth for the past century. Over the years, Enterprise has adopted two mottos: City of Progress and Retirement City U.S.A. The latter moniker has been significantly impacted by military retirees from Fort Rucker, which is less than 10 miles from town.

At the time of Buford Lolley's murder, Enterprise was home to between 15,000 and 16,000 people. Those numbers, however, were somewhat misleading. Many military personnel who were stationed at Fort Rucker, along with their families, actually lived within the city limits of Enterprise. In1968, during the height of the Vietnam War, some 14,000 pilots and support staff were actively engaged in aviation training at the nearby army base.

Consequently, the number of true home folks, including family, friends, acquaintances, and people who were at least familiar by name, face, or reputation, were a smaller subset of the population. As late as 1968, the community maintained a relative measure of serenity and innocence. Illicit drugs, with the exception of small amounts of marijuana, had not yet invaded

Enterprise. There were neither anti-Vietnam war protestors nor an organized hippie counterculture. Despite the chaos erupting throughout much of the country, the boll weevil city was still a relatively tight-knit community.

Then, in mid-January of 1968, a brutal murder disrupted Enterprise's tranquility.

CHAPTER 3

Uncle Bu

I T IS UNFORGIVABLE AND INHUMANE TO forget that murder victims were real people, beloved by their families and closest friends. However, few of Buford Lolley's contemporaries are alive today. By now, if he was still living, he would be 104 years old. With the assistance of surviving family members and a handful of Enterprise residents, most of whom were a generation younger than Lolley, it has been possible to construct at least a skeletal biography of the man whose life ended in such a brutal fashion.

Buford Ervin Lolley was born on July 23, 1916, somewhere in Geneva County, Alabama, located about 25 miles south of Enterprise. At some point, Buford's family relocated closer to Enterprise proper. He was the second oldest of seven children born to John C. and Georgia G. Lolley. From oldest to youngest, the children who survived until adulthood were named Reuben, Buford, Pauline, Mary, Earl, and Robert. A seventh sibling, Gladys Louise, was born when Buford was six years old but died of unknown causes when she was five; her exact position in the birth order of the Lolley siblings is regrettably not recalled.

Little is known about Buford's childhood. His sister-in-law, Mavis, believes his formal education ended before high school. Devout Pentecostals, the Lolley family banned alcohol and television from their home. Buford remained a life-long bachelor and apparently had no long-term romantic relationships.

"I don't think he ever dated," Mavis Lolley recalled years later.

By adulthood, Buford was a likeable, unassuming blue-collar worker. His cousin, Ray, a state senator, was likely his most well-known kinsman.

When John C. Lolley died in 1953, Buford, who was 37 years old, "took over his father's place in the family" and "cared for his mother" for the remainder of his life, according to Mavis. Employed full time, Buford took responsibility for paying the bills and purchasing the groceries. For several years, Buford, his mother, his sister Pauline, and brother Earl lived in the family home on the southern outskirts of Enterprise on Highway 27, which most locals call the Geneva Highway. Years later, after new highway construction and reconfiguration of existing roads, the address for what the Lolley family called the "old home place" changed to 4805 Boll Weevil Circle.

After Earl was discharged from the Army and married a woman from Georgia, the young couple started their own family. At some point as the house grew more crowded, Earl bought out his siblings' shares in the homestead. Now the sole proprietor of the family home, Earl, who worked full-time at nearby Fort Rucker, never had time to operate a full-scale farm but did tend a few cattle and opened the property's fishpond for public use.

Forced to relocate, Buford purchased a house at 730 Bellwood Road, on the southern edge of Enterprise. Georgia Lolley joined her son and daughter, Pauline, in the move. Their new residence was a single-story wood-frame house, painted white and featuring a full-length front porch. Buford would live at the house on Bellwood Road for the remainder of his life.

Of average height with a portly physique, Buford was by no means unattractive. Mavis Lolley particularly remembered his "pretty wavy dark-black hair," which he kept neatly combed in place with the aid of hair oil. Posed alongside his mother in a photograph likely taken in the late 1950s or early 1960s, Buford resembles the actor and comedian Jackie Gleason. While his standard work outfit was overalls, in this snapshot, perhaps taken after church one Sunday, Buford is neatly dressed in pleated pants, polished shoes, and a white dress shirt with the sleeves rolled up, holding a partially smoked cigarette.

A man of few words and no children, Buford was nonetheless fond of youngsters. His pants pockets well-stocked with liberally dispersed candy, he was popular with his nieces and nephews, who affectionately called him Uncle Bu. At some point, he acquired another nickname: Shorty.

Buford's nephew, Michael, offered a lasting memory of his unassuming uncle: "I recall him being quiet and collecting Golden Flake potato chip bags because they awarded points that could be redeemed."

As the head of a small household, Buford maintained steady employment, preferring late-night shifts. Mavis Lolley, whose husband, Robert, served in the military and was often stationed at distant locations, remembered visiting her mother-in-law in Enterprise. During those trips, she distinctly recalled Buford was "either at work or asleep."

With his limited education, Buford was largely restricted to employment in the service industry. For a brief time, he worked for the state of Alabama in an unknown capacity. Afterward, he was a night-shift attendant at the drive-through icehouse in downtown Enterprise. At some point in his late 30s, Buford began working as the overnight attendant at Leon Devane's Save-Way gas station.

Driving an old pickup truck or his jet black, white-topped Pontiac, Buford would leave home late in the evening and head to work. In that era, he likely worked six or seven days a week. The drive from his house to the gas station was conveniently short, just over half a mile.

Despite the violent end to his life, Buford was not one to hold grudges or accumulate enemies. By no means was he considered intimidating in appearance or demeanor.

"He was not that type person," Mavis Lolley recalled.

The adjective most often used to describe Buford was "trusting." A long-time Enterprise resident recalled Buford as being a "good guy" and a "worker bee." That same individual remembered Buford's "pleasant demeanor," noting he "was not a rough neck" and "everybody liked him."

Ricky Adams, a present-day reporter and columnist for *The Enterprise Ledger*, succinctly captured the essence of men like Lolley: "In that era, most every gas station had someone like Buford working. They were hard workers who expected to work six days a week, thankful for having a job. They were the kind of guys I liked and got to know. Most of them told good stories and were friendly, especially if you asked them how they were doing."

Vance Devane, the son of the Save-Way owner, was young when Lolley worked for his father. Years later, he recalled that Buford was "kind and loyal." Vance also remembered his father "had a very hard time finding someone to replace him" after Lolley was killed.

"Buford was as loyal as anyone you ever knew," Vance recalled years later.

Billie Patrick, a long-time resident of Enterprise, characterized Lolley as "so nice and humble." She further described him as "heavy set, slow walking, and easy going." In early January of 1968, roughly a week before Lolley was murdered, Patrick, a 42-year-old wife and mother, stopped at the Save-Way station accompanied by a close friend.

After pumping only 50 cents worth of gas into her car, Buford took the liberty of asking, "Where are you ladies headed?"

"To the beach," Billie jokingly replied.

In 1975, former Alabama Congressman Terry Everett, who at the time was a journalist for *The Daily Ledger*, wrote a series of articles about the seven-year-old unsolved murder of the Save-Way gas station attendant. The journalist offered a succinct description of the murder victim.

"Buford 'Shorty' Lolley was an easy-going fellow who didn't believe in causing a fuss, just treating everyone the same and getting along with everyone he could," Everett reported.

Ken Hooks, one of two attorneys who would later represent the man accused of murdering Lolley, "never heard a bad thing" about the victim's character. Perhaps naïve, Buford was reliable, loyal, and likeable.

The man described by his sister-in-law as a "good person" ultimately met a brutal end. Mavis Lolley said that after Buford was savagely murdered, his mother "grieved herself to death." Her recollection was most accurate and telling.

On December 28, 1968, only 11 months and 14 days after Buford was killed, 70-year-old Georgia Lolley passed away at Gibson Hospital, survived by two daughters, three sons, 17 grandchildren, and six great-grandchildren.

CHAPTER 4

A senseless crime

J.P. STRICKLAND, WHO NORMALLY MANNED THE evening shift at the Save-Way gas station, stayed later than usual on the night of Saturday, January 13, 1968. As best as he could remember, he didn't leave work until the early hours of Sunday around 1:30 a.m.

"It was a real cold night. There was ice that night," Strickland later told newspaper reporters.

He also remembered giving Buford Lolley what was probably the last of many unheeded warnings: "We counted some money and put it in lockup, and I did tell him he should keep the gun that stayed with the station out of the lockup."

"Nothing will ever happen here," Buford innocently replied.

Law enforcement would later determine Lolley was killed during a 22-minute window in the wee hours of Sunday morning. Enterprise Police Department Corporal Junior Faris initiated the fatal timeline when he drove by the Save-Way at 3:15 a.m. and saw Lolley very much alive, standing inside the building.

Fifteen minutes earlier, Lieutenant J.B. McDaniel and his night patrol partner had also driven by the gas station at 716 South Main Street and caught a glimpse of Buford sitting inside. At 3:37 a.m., McDaniel and his partner actually stopped at the Save-Way.

"I got a break between drunks running up and down the road, and since I always stopped to buy a candy bar from Mr. Lolley, I pulled into the station," McDaniel remembered.

McDaniel was appalled by what he discovered: "I walked into the door and noticed something was wrong. There was blood on the floor, and the door had the glass broke out. Blood left a trail behind the counter, and I followed the blood, and Mr. Lolley's body was there on the floor with his head burst open, and the blood was flowing out."

"He had been robbed, and the cash register was open," McDaniel added, attributing motive to the heinous crime.

The police lieutenant immediately knew there had been a struggle as the murder unfolded. In addition to the bloody trail, he noted a hole had been hacked into the building's side door, presumably a missed blow from some kind of heavy weapon, while Lolley was "beaten down to the floor." The attendant's body was discovered behind the merchandise counter in the back right of the building. Lolley had almost made it to the shelf where the pistol was stored in the lockbox before succumbing to his fatal injuries.

Stunned and unable to locate the murder weapon, McDaniel immediately followed protocol: "I stepped back to the car and called for assistance."

Forty-seven-year-old Edward Howard Murdock, Enterprise's chief of police, was among the first summoned to the murder scene. A local resident who knew Murdock, described him as "a good old boy" who had been appointed chief of police by the mayor. A local citizen with close ties to the police department described Murdock as someone who "knew everybody in town and particularly aimed to please the more affluent and politically powerful ones." This profile was not meant to be unflattering, just a common occurrence in many small towns.

After the police chief arrived at the Save-Way, he notified the Alabama Safety Office (later renamed the Alabama Bureau of Investigation) in Montgomery about the murder. State law enforcement investigators arrived on the scene within hours and would subsequently play a crucial role in the search for the killer. Meanwhile, in a failed effort to immediately apprehend the perpetrator, local law enforcement officers and Alabama state troopers set up roadblocks in the Enterprise area.

The state and local lawmen determined Lolley had been bludgeoned to death. The injuries were clearly not survivable.

"Half of his head was hacked away," Chief Murdock recalled.

Later in the day, an undertaker from Searcy Funeral Home obtained a picture of Buford from the decedent's house, not only to make a positive identification of the victim but also to use as a template for cosmetic reconstruction of his battered skull. Lolley's injuries were so gruesome that family members living in Enterprise would not tell his brother, Robert, any specific details about the murder until the family had completed their long drive from the New Jersey military base where he was stationed. Guy Purnell, the state toxicologist who performed the autopsy, determined Lolley had been struck several times on his head and suffered a single blow to his left arm.

Save-Way owner Leon Devane was awakened by a telephone call from the police informing him Lolley had been murdered. Devane's son, Vance, who was 12 years old at the time, later remembered that tragic morning "like it was yesterday." Vance had asked his father what he most remembered when he arrived at the Save-Way after the police contacted him.

"I thought the station was filled with smoke, but it was the steam rising from Buford's body," Devane grimly informed his son.

That same morning, state investigator J.R. Pate and toxicologist Guy Purnell discovered the murder weapon across the street from the gas station, where it had apparently been discarded on the roof of the single-story Enterprise Laundry, also known as Walker's Dry Cleaners. The crude instrument, shaped like a meat cleaver, had been cut from a 3/8th-inch-thick sheet of steel using an acetylene torch. Coffee County Sheriff H.D. Tillman described the exact dimensions of the weapon as "11.5 inches long and 3.5 inches wide." Much to the disappointment of law enforcement agents, there were no fingerprints on the weapon. Nonetheless, Purnell was certain "beyond a doubt" the heavy metal instrument had been used to murder Lolley.

Over the years, some have speculated that the steel used to construct the weapon came from the building site of the new city hall, which was located nearby and in its final phases of construction. Investigators also checked out construction sites in two other South Alabama towns, one in Ozark and the other in Evergreen, both known to have used the same gauge steel, but neither lead proved conclusive. Long-time Enterprise native Ricky Adams, who cannot remember exactly when and where he examined the murder weapon, was certain it had been crafted from the steel used to replace rotting and damaged wooden pickup truck beds at his father's car lot. Identical sheets of steel were routinely stacked behind the Dick Adams Dodge dealership on South Main Street, within easy walking distance of the murder scene.

In his initial comments to newspaper reporters, Chief Murdock stated the murder victim "staggered from the station door to a corner where the body was found." Lolley simply had no ready means of escape.

"They just jumped on him and beat him. He didn't have a chance," the chief glumly added.

Murdock reported that an unknown sum of money was taken from the cash register, but the thieves had apparently overlooked $300 stored in the locked cash box. The chief also revealed that a two-dollar bill given to Lolley by his mother and four silver coins dating back to the 1800s were stolen from the victim's wallet. At the time, a two-dollar bill was a collectible of sorts, having been removed from circulation in 1966.

Murdock also indicated a nearby witness heard a man's voice at or around the time of the murder, pleading: "Help, help, help me!"

Eventually, investigators determined that about $290 was stolen from the cash register, which was opened after the thieves punched in a fictitious 17-cent sale, along with $200 that was taken from Lolley's wallet. In addition to leaving behind the money that was in the lockbox, the perpetrators did not steal any of the coins that were inside the cash register drawer.

By even the laxest of standards, the crime scene was poorly secured. Eighteen-year-old Ricky Adams arrived at the First Methodist Church on South Main Street that same Sunday morning and quickly learned the shocking news about Lolley's murder. Along with a buddy, Adams "skipped Sunday school" and drove to the nearby Save-Way station, which was being guarded by local police. In what was most assuredly a breach of protocol, the lawmen allowed Adams and his friend to enter the building. The victim's body had already been removed, but Adams later vividly recalled an abundance of "blood and clumps of hair."

Fifty-three years later, Adams' recollections remained vivid: "It was a grisly and brutal scene. I wouldn't want to witness it again."

Within days, rewards were being offered in hopes of assisting authorities in solving Lolley's murder. An Associated Press article in the Tuesday, January 16th, issue of *The Montgomery Advertiser* reported that Alabama Governor Lurleen Wallace, at the request of 12th Judicial Circuit District

Attorney Lewey L. Stephens, Jr., had posted "$1,000 state reward money for information leading to the person or persons who killed the night manager of an Enterprise service station." Other reward money was posted, including $100 from the Alabama Petroleum Council, $1,000 from the Enterprise Banking Company, $200 from the Enterprise City Council (the maximum allowed by state law), and $50 from Save-Way owner Leon Devane. That same day, *The Enterprise Ledger* reported that "suspects from Georgia to Florida are being checked out by local and state officials."

After learning additional details about the investigation, the local newspaper informed readers that Lolley may have had a brief forewarning that he was about to be attacked. The account of the assault was horrid.

On January 18th, four days after the murder, *The Enterprise Ledger* reported: "It is also believed that the struggle developed in front of the station; that Lolley attempted to close and lock the door; that the windowpane was knocked out and the door opened while Lolley attempted to reach either the telephone or his gun."

The newspaper also described the trail of blood leading from the front door to the shelf where the pistol was locked away. During the brutal assault, Lolley was repeatedly bludgeoned, as evidenced by blood spatters on the walls and the side door along with a sizable pool of blood on the floor where he collapsed. In that same article, Chief Murdock updated readers about two clues that had already been investigated: a car in Andalusia (a town 44 miles to the west), which proved to be unconnected to the case, and "a trip to DeFuniak Springs, Florida [in the state's panhandle region] that didn't pan out."

Vance Devane later recalled that an ABI investigator told his father he might have been the intended target of the robbers and the murderer. Leon arrived at his gas station at 4:30 a.m. every day, just an hour or so after Lolley was murdered. Moreover, Leon was known to carry $3,000 to $4,000 in his wallet. According to Vance, the wallet was long and well-worn, and the clasp would not close, so it was easy for observers to see money protruding from the end of the billfold in Leon's hip pocket, which made it obvious that the service station owner carried a considerable amount of cash.

On January 20th, Chief Murdock held a formal press conference at the Enterprise Community Center, announcing that the police department was "still not able to pinpoint the person or persons" responsible for the murder of

Buford Lolley. Murdock, however, almost immediately contradicted himself by reporting that two men, thought to be in their late teens or early 20s, were considered the "prime suspects." Unnamed witnesses reported that the young men were seen in the vicinity of the gas station shortly before the murder. The first suspect was described as approximately five-feet, nine-inches-tall, medium built, and wearing a knee-length "sandy all-weather coat." The second suspect, described by Murdock as "slightly heavier but not quite as tall," was reportedly clad in a brown fleece-lined jacket.

Murdock concluded his press conference with an appeal to the citizenry: "I can't believe that someone didn't see them, and I can't believe that people are so callous that they won't say something about it to somebody if they have information that will help us."

Investigators also speculated that Lolley was trying to access the telephone or retrieve the pistol inside the lockbox while he was being beaten to death. During the struggle, the building's plywood side door was splattered with blood and damaged by a misdirected blow from the steel weapon. In addition, law enforcement officials theorized that the suspects who robbed and murdered Lolley lived in the Enterprise area and that the victim likely knew their identities.

In the January 23rd issue of *The Enterprise Ledger*, Sergeant B.J. Gatlin, an 18-year veteran of the Alabama Department of Safety who had spent the past eight years working as an investigator, reported Lolley's murder was "among the most brutal" he had ever investigated. Two days later, the newspaper reminded readers Chief Murdock had promised to keep the identities of any potential witnesses confidential.

On Tuesday, February 6th, *The Enterprise Ledger* reported Chief Murdock and state investigator Sergeant B.J. Gatlin escorted two young men to the state capital at some point during the past weekend. While in Montgomery, the unidentified suspects were administered lie detector tests. After spending "several hours" attached to the polygraph machine, the pair were released without being charged.

Nearly two months after Lolley was killed, *The Enterprise Ledger* gave readers a more precise tally of the money that had been stolen when Lolley was murdered. The thieves swiped $290 from the cash register, $200 from his wallet, and Lolley's prized two-dollar bill. The article neglected to mention the four valuable silver coins pilfered from Lolley's person but did report that

$300 was left behind in the lockbox that contained the pistol. The newspaper reporter added an additional detail: blood stains were left behind on the front doorknob and the left side of the building.

In the weeks and months following Buford Lolley's murder, law enforcement rounded up other potential suspects and took them to ABI headquarters in Montgomery, where they were interrogated and subjected to polygraph tests. Twenty-six-year-old Ned Howell and his friend Doyle Slaughter were two of the so-called suspects.

Howell later recalled that each of them was placed in separate rooms for questioning, but the investigators would rotate back and forth, attempting to uncover any inconsistencies in their stories. According to Howell, Slaughter, who was squeamish by nature, nearly fainted when he was shown a photograph of Lolley's body.

Billie Patrick, a long-time resident of Enterprise, was friends with Ned Howell's sister. According to Patrick, Howell "was scared to death" during the interrogations and polygraph testing.

"It worried him that others might think he did it," Patrick recalled.

Howell had no known history of any criminal offenses or reputation for rowdiness. Both men were soon cleared of wrongdoing and released by state investigators.

It turned out that Howell and Slaughter were repairing an automobile engine in the general vicinity of South Main Street on the afternoon before Lolley's murder. In retrospect, it appears both of them were targeted as potential suspects based on propinquity alone. In the wake of the murder, law enforcement apparently focused on young men largely based on their proximity to the Save-Way station, their past criminal records, or their shady reputations in the community.

On Thursday, January 16, 1969, a year and two days after the murder, *The Enterprise Ledger* reported "the Enterprise police and state investigators are still at work, seeking the murderers of Buford E. Lolley." Chief Murdock informed readers that he planned to "to arrange a lie-detector test on another suspect in the case." The police chief also indicated that "several names" had been removed from the list of suspects, narrowing the search. Other than Ned Howell and Doyle Slaughter, the names of the other suspects who were interrogated and polygraphed remain unknown.

At the same time, Murdock stated he "would still like to hear from anyone who has additional information in the case." In conclusion, the reporter wrote, the chief "still believes the culprits will be brought to justice."

In reality, 12 months after Buford Lolley's murder, the investigation was stone cold.

CHAPTER 5

A suspect in the making

D<small>AVID</small> H<small>UTTO, THE MAN WHO WOULD</small> eventually be indicted, arrested, tried, and acquitted for the murder of Buford Lolley, was born on August 27, 1948, in Abbeville, Alabama, located approximately 49 miles northeast of Enterprise near the Georgia state line. He was the second youngest of seven children born to Noah Thomas (Tom) and Ida Inez Braswell Hutto. After living for a short while in both Abbeville and Florida, the Hutto family moved to Enterprise when David was a child.

Family members recall Tom Hutto as quiet and willful but never abusive toward his wife and children. He had no known criminal record. He was, however, a heavy drinker and died of a heart attack at the age of 53, just two days before David's 13th birthday.

According to David's wife, Susan, he was essentially "raised by his mother" and remembered his childhood as "happy." Inez Hutto, who lived to be 79, remained devoted to David throughout his life. In turn, he fit the role of a prototypical mama's boy.

Brown-haired and blue-eyed, David had a slight build. As an adult, he stood five-feet, seven-inches-tall and weighed, by generous estimates, only 130 pounds. While never averse to work and described by many as quite intelligent, he dropped out of school in the 10th or 11th grade. His wife attributed his shortened education to repeated truancy and recalled that David once told her that a teacher had said he was "smart enough to be a doctor."

On Hutto's final report card for the 1960–1961 school year, when he completed sixth grade, his teacher, Mrs. J.R. Snellgrove, wrote: "David does not bring in his homework. He should make better grades. I have enjoyed having David in my room. He needs to stay in school more, as he could be a good student."

Truancy, however, remained a problem. At the end of one nine-week period during his seventh-grade year, David's report card recorded 14½ days present and 15½ days absent. In the end, he simply lacked the discipline or the interest to apply himself to academics.

Bernadette Susan Simmons was 19 years old when she met David Hutto. The first time she encountered her husband-to-be, Susan was staying with her sister and brother-in-law, who lived just north of Enterprise. The romance began at a gas station, where Susan admittedly flirted with David by urging him to turn up the volume on his car radio.

Having been raised in a "Christian family," Susan considered 21-year-old David, who regularly consumed alcohol and chain-smoked cigarettes, to be "a challenge" and was uncharacteristically attracted to his "wild side." The couple's courtship was whirlwind. After a first date on August 27, 1971, they wed less than two months later. Even though their engagement was brief, the Huttos' marriage lasted for nearly 45 years until David's death in early 2016.

The newlyweds lived in David's mother's house on Mill Street in Enterprise. For a time, his brother, Roy, also resided at Inez Hutto's home. For nearly 20 years, David and Susan would remain under the roof of his mother's various rental homes until Inez died in April of 1990.

Although he was short and rail thin, David was strong for his size and began his work career as a roofer. His choice of occupations clearly reinforces the axiom that size does not always matter, as anyone who has ever carried a slab of shingles up a ladder can attest. Roofing houses and commercial buildings is strenuous labor, particularly during blistering hot and oppressively humid summers in Lower Alabama.

From the beginning of their marriage, David was "very loving and very protective," Susan later recalled. She also described David as "calm and easy going" with a long fuse.

"It took a lot to get him upset," she said, "but if you talked bad about his family, he'd whip your ass."

Former District Judge and District Attorney Gary McAliley remembered Hutto "wouldn't take crap from anyone, but also wouldn't look for a fight." While many locals acknowledged he was considered one of Enterprise's young rowdies, none recall being frightened by him.

David was a skilled billiards player. While still a teenager, he once defeated a talented pool player in the nearby town of Geneva. Ironically, the youth who was the victim of David's billiards prowess on that particular day, Steve Weekley, would later arrest Hutto and charge him with murder.

Ricky Adams, a long-time Enterprise resident, was familiar with the acknowledged pool shark. He played with Hutto at Marsh's Snooker and Eat on South Main Street, recalling decades later that David was a "good snooker player."

Adams also remembered Hutto's severe strabismus, commonly known as a lazy eye: "I didn't know which way he was looking."

Years later, Hutto would have his weakened eye muscles surgically corrected. From that point forward, he was able to maintain continuous and direct eye contact.

Never sensing any violent tendencies in Hutto, Adams recalled: "I don't remember him starting any fights."

Susan gave birth to a daughter, Kimberly Sue, in 1972 and a son, Christopher David, in 1973. It is also possible that Hutto may have fathered a child out of wedlock. Kim Hutto Mitchell said that a woman claiming to be her half-sister made contact via social media. After Kim travelled to North Alabama for a face-to-face meeting with her alleged half-sibling, the woman suddenly and without explanation refused to meet with her. Consequently, it is not known if the mysterious woman was actually fathered by David.

Billy Wayne Bradley was among David's known youthful associates. Born on August 28, 1944, to James G. Bradley and Mary Alice Sims Bradley, Billy Wayne was an only child and one day shy of being four years older than David Hutto. Bradley was bulkier than the rail-thin Hutto: five-feet, nine-inches-tall and weighing approximately 200 pounds. Like David, Billy Wayne apparently never finished high school, probably a result of truancy, academic failure, and frank indifference.

Billie Patrick, who lived on Rawls Street in Enterprise when she was a child, was a year or two younger than Billy Wayne. Billie's parents owned their home, and the Bradley family lived in a rental duplex next door. She clearly recalled that Billy Wayne was "mean to me and my sister." If he could not force the young girls to eat the mud pies they were making in their own yard, Billy Wayne would instead throw them at Billie and her sister. On other occasions, she said, young Bradley would "push us over when we were riding our bicycles."

While she acknowledged Billy Wayne was a "nice looking boy," Billie said her parents did not want the Patrick siblings to "associate with him" because of his nasty disposition. She also recalled that the Bradley family rarely had any visitors, including kinfolk. Billie's father, a municipal judge, told his daughter he "was not surprised" when Billy Wayne started getting into trouble with the law during his teen years.

Most Enterprise residents who knew Bradley remembered him working as a house painter, though at least one contemporary thought he might also have been employed as an electrician. He was also seen from time to time working at his father's machine shop in the South Main Street area, within easy walking distance of the Save-Way gas station.

After Susan married David, Bradley remained her husband's friend, she said, but he was never a "good friend." She distinctly remembered how much Bradley "liked to drink" and his showing up at their house "drunk as a jailhouse dog."

How close were Hutto and Bradley in 1968, the year of Buford Lolley's murder and more than three years before David met his future wife? The intimacy of their friendship is not fully known, but more than one Enterprise resident remembers the two of them as being among a group of rowdies who regularly "hung out" together.

There was, however, at least one critical difference in the personalities of the two young men. While Hutto was not known to seek out violent confrontations, Bradley was volatile and frequently looked for fights. One local resident, four years younger than Billy Wayne, remembered that Bradley was "meaner than hell" and was "looking for trouble all the time." More than once, this same youth was warned by his parents to "stay away" from Bradley.

Eddie Lammon, a husky high-school football player and a future veterinarian, recalled two incidents that illuminated Bradley's character and demeanor. Lammon remembered Billy Wayne repeatedly "messing with" him when they were in school together. Billy Wayne's verbal taunts eventually led to a physical altercation on the grounds of what was then known as Coffee

County High School, the predecessor to Enterprise High School. The scuffle ended with Lammon twice pinning Bradley to the ground and pressing his face in the dirt before Billy Wayne finally promised to end his taunting.

On another occasion, Eddie was fishing at an area lake. Using a new type of artificial bait, Lammon reeled in a four-pound bass, the biggest fish he had ever caught. Bradley, who happened to be at the lake when Lammon landed his catch, not only wanted Eddie to give him the fish, but also insisted on receiving credit for catching the bass. As might have been expected, Lammon refused to accede to Billy Wayne's demands but cited this incident as a prime example of Bradley's "attention-seeking" personality.

A retired Enterprise Police Department officer recalled a striking difference between the two young men. He remembered that Bradley was prone to seeking trouble, while "Hutto was a follower."

"David Hutto was worried about his own well-being and could not take pressure," the former lawman opined.

Former Judge Gary McAliley has long believed that Bradley was capable of committing violence "in a flash." The stark difference in the temperaments of Hutto and Bradley has proven crucial when re-examining the murder of Buford Lolley.

In his younger days, David Hutto was not exactly a candidate for sainthood. After the couple was married, Susan was only partially aware of her husband's criminal history.

However, she never pushed him to disclose any of his past misdeeds: "What he did before we met was his business."

The only crime she recalled David admitting to occurred when he and his close friend "Runt" Qualls were arrested and incarcerated for stealing hogs they supposedly discovered running free on the side of the road. In truth, before he was married, David had other arrests, all but one apparently related to offenses where he did not physically harm anyone else.

After they were married, David's difficulties with the legal system were limited to numerous arrests for driving under the influence of alcohol, Susan recalled. More than once, he spent the night in jail after being charged with DUI. Susan clearly remembered the police following her when she was behind the wheel of their car, stopping her as close as a half-mile from their home "thinking it was David driving, instead of me."

In Susan's opinion, David had become a "household name" to local law enforcement officers. She was also convinced that the Enterprise Police Department had long-since labeled him a "bad guy."

Did Hutto's less-than-stellar reputation lead to eventual misidentification as a killer, or would he later be used by law enforcement as bait to capture Buford Lolley's actual murderer?

CHAPTER 6

The media revival

IN MARCH OF 1975, JUST OVER seven years after Buford Lolley was killed, *The Daily Ledger* and radio station WIRB ran a series of newspaper articles and news broadcasts, intent on reviving local interest in the cold-case murder. From the beginning, newspaper readers and radio listeners were made aware that $2,350 in reward money was available for those willing to provide new information about who might be responsible for Lolley's violent death.

The media effort, driven by journalist Terry Everett and radio newsman Bernie Cobb, was certainly welcomed by law enforcement. Since the newspaper articles contained information not previously revealed to the public, it appears Everett and Cobb were granted access to the Lolley murder investigation files compiled by the Enterprise Police Department and/or the Alabama Bureau of Investigation. Forty-six years later, neither of the principals in the media revival were able to share their recollections. Cobb died in February of 2000, and Everett, through an intermediary, reported no specific memories about writing the newspaper columns or the events leading up to their publication.

Born on February 15, 1937, in Dothan, Alabama, Everett graduated high school in 1955. As a member of the United States Air Force, he was assigned duties as an intelligence analyst. Afterward, he spent some 30 years in journalism, as both a reporter and a publisher. Everett later became involved in other business endeavors, including ownership of a residential construction company. In 1992, he was elected to the first of eight consecutive terms in the United States House of Representatives, representing Alabama's Second Congressional District.

Bernie Cobb was born on January 20, 1929, and later served as a lieutenant colonel in the United States Army. In 1975, Cobb was a well-respected WIRB radio newsman. He would later serve for 14 years as the public relations and marketing director for the Medical Center of Enterprise.

Thirty-eight years old in 1975, Everett wrote several articles for *The Daily Ledger* concerning the Lolley cold case. As a result, fellow citizens learned more about Lolley's murder.

On Friday, March 14th, he reported: "Buford Lolley died January 14, 1968—seven years ago. Whoever is responsible for the brutal murder remains free. Since this series of articles and reports on WIRB started a week ago, several new leads have developed in the Lolley case. These leads are being held in confidence by the news media and authorities. Where will they lead? Will they lead to the killers of Buford Lolley? Only time will tell. Authorities are hopeful that anyone else having any information on the case will contact them by some means."

The articles published in *The Daily Ledger* seamlessly rehashed information published at the time of murder, alongside new details about the brutal crime. The newspaper also featured photographs of the Save-Way gas station, the murder weapon, and a view of the nearby street where previously unreported eyewitnesses saw two suspects fleeing the scene of the crime. In addition, the newspaper published a diagram of the interior layout of the station, including the position of the victim's body.

J.P. Strickland, the Save-Way gas station's early night-shift attendant, was among those interviewed by the newspaper. Just hours before the murder, he had advised Buford Lolley to keep the station's .32 caliber pistol in his pocket for easy access rather than storing it in the lockbox.

"Nothing will ever happen here," Lolley innocently replied.

"I told him there was a first time for anything, but he still wouldn't believe that anyone would ever hurt him and nothing like that would ever happen, so he left it in the lockup," Strickland remembered.

On Wednesday, March 12th, the local newspaper informed readers that two young men "in their late teens or early twenties" were seen running away from the Save-Way gas station at around 3:30 a.m. on January 14, 1968. One of the two stopped briefly, about 15 feet down Erin Street, which ran perpendicular to South Main, and tossed an object on top of the Enterprise Laundry, located at the junction of the two streets.

At 3:37 a.m., just minutes after the two young men departed the gas station on foot, Enterprise Police Department Lieutenant J.B. McDaniel and his partner stopped at the Save-Way. As reported at the time of the murder, McDaniel often bought a candy bar from Lolley during his brief work break. It had been a busy night for the two policemen since the beginning of their shift at 10:00 p.m. on that Saturday, having already charged 11 motorists with driving under the influence.

As he approached the front door of the station, McDaniel grew uneasy: "I walked into the door and noticed something was wrong. Blood was on the floor, and the door had glass broke in it. The blood left a trail going behind the counter, and I followed it. Mr. Lolley was laying there with his head all burst open and the blood flowing out."

After noticing that the cash register drawer was open, McDaniel "knew he had been robbed" and immediately absorbed his surroundings: "There had been a fight there. There had been a hole knocked in the front door and also the side door where they beat Mr. Lolley down the wall. I stepped back to the car and called for assistance."

Despite the passage of time, the grisly scene had left an indelible impression on McDaniel: "One side of his head was completely beaten off."

As the crime scene was processed, other markers of violence were discovered. McDaniel later recalled that blood was found on the front doorknob and the outside wall of the gas station.

Police Chief Howard Murdock informed Everett how he learned about the brutal crime: "Normally, I would be notified by the desk of a murder, but I was in my office that morning."

After the dispatcher received McDaniel's urgent radio broadcast, the information was immediately relayed to the chief. When he arrived at the Save-Way station, Murdock was stunned by the macabre scene.

"I guess my first thought was how vicious the attack had been. It was brutal; one lick would have killed Mr. Lolley, but you could tell there had been a struggle, and he had been beaten senselessly," the police chief recalled.

As darkness gave way to daybreak on that Sunday morning, state investigators from Montgomery arrived at the murder scene. After examining

Lolley's body and the surrounding area, state law enforcement agents concluded the murder weapon was "a heavy, blunt object."

State investigator J.R. "Skeeter" Pate was convinced that the murderer discarded the weighty weapon "as soon as possible." It did not take long for Pate and state toxicologist Guy Purnell to locate the cleaver-like weapon across the street from the gas station on the roof of the Enterprise Laundry.

The newspaper also reminded readers that four silver dollars dating back to the 1800s and a two-dollar bill, both stolen from Lolley's wallet, had yet to be discovered. The wallet was thought to have been removed from the victim's pocket by one of the perpetrators as he lay dead or dying on the concrete floor of the service station.

A day later, *The Daily Ledger* reported that Buford Lolley's dying pleas were heard by two witnesses who lived in a house on the opposite side of South Main Street from the scene of the murder. At the request of law enforcement, the newly reported witnesses, a husband and wife, were given pseudonyms, Mr. and Mrs. X. Two years later, their actual names would be revealed in a courtroom. On the night of January 13, 1968, the couple watched television most of the evening and specifically recalled tuning into their favorite program, *Mission Impossible*.

Around 11:30 p.m., Mr. and Mrs. X decided to retire for the evening, but as Everett noted, neither could fall asleep: "They had tossed and turned, talked, and smoked a cigarette or two."

Sometime after 3:00 a.m., Mr. X clearly heard voices coming from the gas station across the street, which was not an infrequent occurrence. On this particular occasion, however, the words were unusually "low and soft."

Furthermore, he distinctly recalled a man pleading: "Help, help, help me!"

Even though Mrs. X was lying in bed next to her husband and could not clearly make out the exact content of the words, both were concerned enough to peer outside their bedroom window. The couple noted the door to the Save-Way was open but did not immediately see anyone in the vicinity of the gas station. Mr. X recalled glancing at his watch as he walked to front of house and looked out the window facing Erin Street—the time was 3:20 a.m. After once again observing nothing untoward, Mr. X returned to the bedroom.

"It's just a couple of teenagers acting the fool," Mrs. X opined to her husband.

Not yet fully convinced by her initial conclusion, Mrs. X decided to look out the bedroom window once again. At this point, she saw a young man coming out the front door of the gas station. He paused briefly and reached back to grab "an unidentified object" from inside the building, using his right hand. After walking to the area where the gas pumps were located, he paused momentarily, waiting for another young man to exit the building. Afterward, the pair walked hurriedly across South Main Street.

By the time Mr. X made it from the front of the house to the bedroom window, the two young men were out of his line of sight. At the time of the media reinvestigation, Mr. X told Everett he never actually saw either one of the alleged suspects, a story he would dramatically alter the following year. Despite what she had seen while peering out the bedroom window a second time, Mrs. X still believed the previous commotion came from "a couple of teenagers out late and cutting up." According to the newspaper article, Mr. and Mrs. X had both passed polygraph tests about what they witnessed in the wee hours of January 14, 1968.

In that same article, Everett reported that Sergeant B.J. Gatlin of the Investigative and Identification Division of the Alabama Department of Public Safety had visited the newspaper's office a day earlier to discuss the cold-case murder. Gatlin informed the journalist that "countless" individuals had been interviewed and that "nine suspects were given polygraph tests." The investigator, however, said that "no positive identification and very few physical clues have kept the killers safe."

Gatlin had already spent many weeks in Enterprise working the Lolley murder case. Still, he was prepared to continue the investigation until the murder was solved.

"I'm available to do the same thing at this time. I'm just as much interested in solving this case as anybody in the world," he informed Everett.

The investigator was just as eager to capture the murderer as he had been in 1968. Gatlin made it clear to local citizens that he would "be willing to talk to anyone at any time."

In the March 14th edition of the newspaper, Everett recalled the unsolved crime occurred around 3:30 a.m. on a bitterly cold day. Prior to Lolley's murder, two young men were seen approaching the Save-Way gas station on foot. One was described as standing approximately five-feet, nine-inches-tall, medium built, "neatly dressed," and wearing a knee-length "sandy color all-weather coat." The second man was reported to be "slightly heavier, but not as tall as his companion" and dressed in a brown fleece-lined corduroy jacket. Since these descriptions of the suspects predated those provided by Mr. and Mrs. X, the newspaper led readers to believe there must have been at least one other witness but never specifically addressed the issue. Over a half-century later, the answer to that question remains unknown.

In the same article, Everett wrote that at least one of the young men "probably wore gloves" and had the bulge of a weapon protruding from the front of his coat. In addition, the journalist wrote, "there is reason to believe that one, or perhaps both of them, had been drinking." The supposition about the gloves could be inferred from the frigid weather conditions and the absence of fingerprints on the murder weapon. Once again, the newspaper did not report how it obtained the information about the bulging weapon and the suspects' potential intoxication.

As the two suspects approached the gas station, Everett surmised: "Lolley could have been dozing in a large, stuffed chair against the back wall of the station but facing the door. In two minutes or less, the pair of intruders entered the building, opened the cash register, and stole the paper money."

But stealing cash was not quite enough. The robbers also pocketed a pack of chewing gum and a piece of candy from the display counter.

The Daily Ledger article speculated about what happened next. Lolley was thought to have awakened, either on his own or after hearing the sound of the cash register opening but before the thieves had exited the front lot of the gas station. After noticing the open register drawer, the attendant, likely concerned about his personal safety, rushed to the front door, closing and locking it. In response to Lolley's sudden movements, the two youths raced back to the door, at which time one of them dropped the stolen package of chewing gum. When they discovered the front door was locked, one of the suspects apparently used the steel weapon to shatter a pane of glass, reached inside, and unlocked the door.

Lolley's first physical encounter with the robbers likely occurred at the station's front entrance where he forcefully tried to hold the door shut. His efforts proved unsuccessful, as evidenced by the beginning of a blood trail near the front door. At some point, a blow was delivered to the underside of Lolley's left wrist, likely defensive in nature, after he positioned his arms in a self-protective posture.

Clearly in fear for his life, Lolley made it to a small counter just inside the front door, where the cash register, a telephone, and a set of keys to the lockbox containing the pistol were located. As the murderer repeatedly struck him in the head with the crude weapon, Lolley staggered backward and dropped the keys to the floor. The bludgeoning continued as the helpless victim tried to escape his assailant. Lolley eventually collapsed on the concrete floor near the back wall of the station "with the left side of his head beaten off."

The murder weapon, discovered later in the day on top of the laundry, was a cleaver-like instrument, 11.5 inches long and 3.5 inches at its greatest width, but failed to yield any fingerprints. According to newspaper reports, the murderous thieves pilfered $290 from the cash register, $200 from Lolley's wallet, and the two-dollar bill that his mother had given him. Though previously reported but not mentioned in this particular article, the victim's four silver coins were also stolen from his billfold.

The Daily Ledger reminded readers that local and state law enforcement investigators had actively worked the case for several weeks after the crime was committed. Aside from the murder weapon, there was very little physical evidence—a fact that would forever plague the case.

The newspaper noted that "some witnesses were reluctant to talk." The absence of eyewitness reports had no doubt hampered the investigation.

"It has been said they feared for their lives and the lives of their families," Everett wrote, before imploring readers: "It is far better to have murderers behind bars than running free in society. It is time the police received all information concerning this case."

The case had remained cold for more than seven years, but 21 months later, an arrest would finally be made.

CHAPTER 7

The arrest

Monday, December 13, 1976, started out like any other day for 28-year-old David Hutto. But shortly before sunset, his world would be turned upside down.

Late in the afternoon, he drove to Chambers Grocery on the Geneva Highway to buy some baby aspirin. Years later, his wife, Susan, could not recall whether it was one of their children, a niece, or a nephew who was sick, which necessitated David's trip to the store.

At 5:25 p.m., just as Hutto reached the grocery checkout, he was arrested by Corporal Steve Weekley of the Alabama Bureau of Investigation and Enterprise Police Chief Howard Murdock. Weekley immediately handcuffed a bewildered David. Susan Hutto later said there had been no forewarning; her husband's arrest "came totally out of the blue."

When Investigator Weekley snapped the handcuffs on him, Hutto offered no resistance but tersely warned the lawman: "You had better know what you're doing."

The arrest came on the same day that Circuit Court Judge Riley Green presided over a grand jury that indicted David Hutto for first-degree murder. After the indictment was returned, Green ordered Hutto's arrest. On December 14th, *The Daily Ledger* headlined: GRAND JURY INDICTS A SUSPECT IN BUFORD LOLLEY MURDER CASE. Local residents could only hope justice was finally being served, nearly nine years after the humble and well-liked gas station attendant had been brutally slain.

Twenty-eight-year-old ABI Investigator Jackie Stephen Weekley was the driving force behind Hutto's indictment and arrest. Born on November 26, 1948, at Fort Still, Oklahoma, he was raised in a military family and grew up in various places, including Salzburg, Austria; Aschaffenburg, Germany; and Gadsden, Alabama. When Weekley was a teenager, his family relocated to Geneva, Alabama, approximately 25 miles south of Enterprise. In 1967, less than a year before Buford Lolley was murdered, Weekley graduated from Geneva Community High School.

After Weekley's father, a sergeant in the United States Army, retired from the military in 1961, he was hired as an Alabama state trooper. By the time he retired in 1989, the elder Weekley had risen to a ranking position in the Safety Education Division.

In August of 1968, Steve Weekley followed in his father's footsteps, joining the Alabama State Troopers as a cadet. He was stationed in the west central Alabama town of Demopolis. In 1969, he was transferred to Dothan, located a bit over 30 miles east of Enterprise. That same year, Weekley enrolled at Enterprise State Junior College and graduated in 1971 with an associate degree. A year later, he was promoted to a full-fledged state trooper. After relocating to Enterprise in late 1972, Weekley began night school at the Fort Rucker branch of Troy State University. In 1974, he earned a bachelor of science degree in psychology and was transferred to the Alabama Bureau of Investigation. Weekley would later complete his master's degree in police science.

Blonde-haired, physically fit, and soft-spoken, Weekley was also intelligent, resourceful, and devoted to his new job as a state investigator. A veteran jurist remembered Weekley had a "warm personality but was very ambitious." A close friend described Weekley as "clever" and "a good investigator."

"He thought he could outsmart any criminal," the same long-time Enterprise resident opined.

Reporting on the indictment and arrest of David Hutto, *The Montgomery Advertiser* quoted Weekley, informing readers he had pursued the murder investigation into "three states" and "several foreign countries." The latter statement was a bit misleading when referencing the word "pursued," as Weekley never actually left the United States during the time he was investigating the Lolley cold-case murder. *The Daily Ledger* also quoted

Weekley, who reported "over 100 witnesses in a number of states and Germany" were questioned as the investigation unfolded.

The hometown newspaper also cited the dying victim's final words as a key factor in the arrest: "Witnesses overheard Lolley's call for help and now have apparently identified Hutto as one of the two young men allegedly seen leaving the station."

On Tuesday, December 14th, *The Dothan Eagle* ran an article about the ABI's involvement in Hutto's apprehension: "The arrest came less than a year after Weekley, formerly a state trooper, was reassigned a criminal investigator and reopened the files on a crime that had seemed almost forgotten."

The newspaper reported the young ABI investigator had become interested in the cold case several months ago. Since that time, he diligently followed every lead.

Chief Murdock gave the lion's share of the credit to Weekley: "He started working on the case in March and has been at it every day since then. Steve is the one who caused the case to break."

According to reporter Tex Middlebrooks: "One by one, Weekley narrowed down his list of suspects and built up what officers considered a good case."

After Weekley took his case to the grand jury on December 13th, an indictment was issued shortly before 5:00 p.m. From there, the state investigator acted immediately, placing Hutto under arrest less than a half hour later. According to *The Daily Ledger* reporter Terry Everett, Weekley gave credit to the newspaper reports and radio broadcasts from March of 1975, which "had renewed public interest in the case."

On Friday, December 17, 1976, Roy Shoffner, the editor of *The Daily Ledger* and a 22-year veteran of the same newspaper, wrote a column entitled "It Took Nine Years." He started out by recalling his own unforgettable experience taking photographs at the Lolley murder scene in January of 1968. Shoffner also cited the newspaper articles and radio broadcasts from a year earlier, which had stirred the public's interest in the case.

"This doesn't mean that the suspect is actually guilty. He remains a suspect. He has been charged. He will face trial before a jury. Only then will the verdict be guilty—or innocent. Only then will he be sentenced as a convicted criminal—or released, exonerated of the charges. But after nine years, after much investigation, some action has developed. The case has been brought back to life. Perhaps, yet, Lolley's murderer will draw the penalty deserved," he concluded.

The Montgomery Advertiser, with a much wider readership than the local newspaper, also publicized Hutto's arrest, describing the 1968 crime as "one of the most brutal murders ever staged in this part of Alabama." Meanwhile, 12th Circuit Court District Attorney Lewey L. Stephens, Jr. adopted a low-key approach, informing the capital city newspaper that any reports about him holding a press conference were "erroneous and that to do so could influence the possible outcome of the trial involving the indicted man."

Absent bond, Hutto was incarcerated at the Coffee County jail in Elba, located 16 miles west-northwest of Enterprise. While her husband was behind bars, Susan was only allowed to see him on Sundays. Though visitation was limited, she faithfully brought David, who was a picky eater, some of his favorite foods, which he readily shared with fellow inmates. On at least one occasion, she provided him a quilt, adding a layer of warmth to the spartan covers on his jailhouse cot.

Kim and Chris Hutto were unable to enter the jail proper and were forced to remain outside while Susan visited their father. David's two young children could only catch glimpses of him as he stood behind a barred window in the jail portion of the Elba County Courthouse.

A photograph taken of Hutto while he was confined in the county jail shows him cleanly shaven with neatly groomed hair. Sitting on a cot covered with a quilt, perhaps the same one brought to him by his wife, Hutto is wearing slacks and a football jersey imprinted with the number 19. In this snapshot, Hutto's countenance is mostly blank, neither over-friendly nor sinister. Pictures of his wife and children along with a calendar are taped on the rear wall of the jail cell.

For the time being, Steve Weekley emerged as a hero of sorts, while David Hutto languished in jail for 103 days, waiting for the start of his murder trial.

CHAPTER 8

The first trial

B OTH OF DAVID HUTTO'S MURDER TRIALS were conducted at the auxiliary county courthouse in Enterprise, located on 99 South Edwards Street, within sight of the town's signature Boll Weevil Monument. For many years leading up to 1977, arguments about the location and the number of courthouses in Coffee County had been the sources of intense debates.

Coffee County was officially established in 1841, and nine years later, Elba was designated as the seat of government. A year later, the first county courthouse was constructed in what became known as Elba's Courthouse Square. In 1863, near the midpoint of the Civil War, the original courthouse was set ablaze by Confederate deserters. Fortunately, most of the records stored in the building were saved from the flames. The present-day Elba county courthouse, erected in 1903, withstood disastrous flooding on more than one occasion during the 20th century after the Pea River levee collapsed during torrential rains, leaving the downtown area underwater. Present-day high-water stains on the interior of the building serve as a visible reminder of the floods.

By the beginning of the 20th century, Enterprise's city limits were expanding, and its population was rapidly growing, soon dwarfing Elba both in size and numbers. In 1907, Coffee County was officially divided into two jurisdictional sections. Consequently, an auxiliary seat of government was established in Enterprise to serve the needs of residents in the eastern part of county.

Since there was no legislation mandating county funding for constructing branch courthouses, Enterprise was initially forced to build a less costly wood frame structure, paid for by local citizens. After just a few years, the first courthouse burned to the ground. In 1920, at the cost of $27,000, a brick courthouse was completed. On January 23, 1924, the second building was also gutted by fire. Some conspiracy-minded Enterprise residents suspected a group of Elba residents turned arsonists, not yet accepting of the need for an auxiliary courthouse in Coffee County, set fire to one or both buildings.

A third auxiliary courthouse was built in 1925, remaining operational for 73 years. With fireproof rooms and safety vaults for all public documents, the newly constructed building was regarded as more than adequate for its time.

By the spring of 1977, when the Hutto case went to trial, Enterprise's auxiliary county courthouse had seen better days. The building was small and overcrowded, and its interior furnishings were worn down by aging.

Visitors to the two-story white brick building, which also included a basement filled with offices, climbed only a few steps before entering the building's small lobby. On the top floor, just above the front entrance, a pair of glass-paned doors opened to a small stoop, not quite big enough to be considered a balcony. In the front center of the courthouse, a column extended well beyond the shingled roof line; the space was originally designed to accommodate an oversized clock, but that addition had not yet been made. At some point between the 1977 murder trial and the building's razing in 1998, an exterior clock was installed on the edifice.

The entrance to the Office of the Clerk of Court, located on the first floor, was protected by an inner wooden door and an outside screened door, the latter featuring a Sunbeam Bread advertisement printed on its exterior handle. The screened entrance was likely a relic from the days gone by, before air conditioning was available. Between opened windows in the clerk's office and the screened door, it may have been possible to create at least a tiny cross draft during the stifling hot summer months.

For ease of cleaning, the oak hardwood floors in the clerk's office and many other areas of the courthouse were covered with linoleum. While the linoleum may have been easier to sweep and mop, the color and design pattern of the floor covering were less than pleasing to the eye.

Four deputy clerks, under the supervision of Clerk of the Court Jim Ellis, sat at desks behind a counter that stretched across the front of the room.

Area attorneys would sometimes encounter one another and socialize for a bit when filing cases in the clerk's office.

The second-floor courtroom was accessible by a single flight of steps served by two stairwells. The stairway was narrow enough to induce panic in claustrophobics. If two people of sufficient bulk were traveling in opposite directions, one of them would have to turn sideways and let the other pass before resuming his or her journey.

The main entrance to the courtroom had a large glass windowpane, gray tinted on the outside and clear on the inside. More functional than ornate, the courtroom's floors were covered with the ubiquitous linoleum. Undecorated plaster walls supported a white-painted tin ceiling. While there were no ceiling fans, air conditioning, which had been installed by 1977, offered relief from the oppressive summertime heat. The only wall adornment was the Great Seal of the State of Alabama, located directly behind the judge's bench. The courtroom's lone set of windows overlooked the building's large rear parking lot.

Trial observers sat in two rows of hardwood benches, six to eight benches per row. Spittoons were strategically positioned for the benefit of tobacco chewers. During the winter months, two large gas-fueled space heaters, positioned equidistantly in front of the rail separating the gallery from the remainder of courtroom, were directed toward the judge's bench. The rail featured a swinging door, allowing lawyers and witnesses to access their respective seats.

The top of the judge's roughly constructed raised wooden bench was partially covered with the same unattractive linoleum used on the floors. Behind the bench, two doors, similar in design and color to the one at the main entrance, led to a hearing room, the judge's chambers, and his judicial assistant's office. As the judge looked out over the courtroom, a desk for the clerk of the court and a holding cell for prisoners were positioned to his right, while the witness chair and jury box were located to his left. The jury box contained 14 chairs, in the rare event two alternates were qualified for jury duty. The prosecutor's table was located closest to the jury box, while the defense attorneys sat on the opposite side of the room. The counsels' tables, approximately eight feet long, were constructed of pine, painted gray, and topped with the seemingly endless linoleum.

The courtroom's lack of a public address system coupled with 16-feet raised ceilings often made it difficult to hear. One judge remembered the "awful acoustics," which sometimes required trial participants to raise their voices and repeat themselves.

Thirty-two-year-old Terry Butts was the circuit judge responsible for presiding over David Hutto's murder trial. A native of Crenshaw County and a graduate of the University of Alabama School of Law, Butts spent the first eight years of his career in private practice in neighboring Elba. Only a year before Hutto's murder trial, Butts was elected as one of two judges in Alabama's 12th Judicial Circuit, which served both Coffee and Pike Counties. Eventually, the growing district would add a third judge.

Butts was five-feet, eleven-inches-tall, with broad shoulders, light brown hair, and blue eyes. Well-read and knowledgeable, Judge Butts sometimes caught people off guard with his witty retorts.

He, like many other circuit judges, did not wear robes in court, heeding the advice of Judge Eris Paul, a revered legend in the 12th circuit: "A judge wearing robes is like dressing up a pig."

Although there was a gavel at hand, Butts rarely used it, taking pride in his ability to maintain an orderly courtroom. To discourage large-scale disruptions by disgruntled defendants or members of the gallery, Judge Butts habitually stationed physically imposing sheriff's deputies and state troopers at strategic positions throughout his courtrooms.

District Attorney Lewey L. Stephens, Jr. and Assistant District Attorney Dale Marsh were responsible for prosecuting David Hutto. With a combination of experience and youthful tenacity, they were formidable advocates for the state.

Stephens, age 52, was an experienced prosecutor, who served as district attorney on two separate occasions over the course of 18 years. In the 1950s, Stephens was asked to assist in the prosecution of Phenix City, Alabama's famed Dixie Mafia. A local gangster, in what was then known as "Sin City," shot and killed Attorney General-Elect Albert Patterson. A native of Phenix City, the newly elected attorney general had run on a campaign pledge to rid the city of vice and corruption. After Patterson was assassinated, his son, John, was elected attorney general in a special election and ultimately fulfilled his late father's wishes, restoring law and order to Phenix City. Patterson's reputation as a crime buster became nationally known after the 1955 release of a major motion picture, entitled *The Phenix City Story*, and eventually led to his being elected governor of Alabama in 1958. Meanwhile, young Stephens' prosecutorial role in Phenix City helped solidify his reputation as a seeker of justice.

Born and raised in nearby New Brockton, Stephens was a World War II veteran and a graduate of the University of Alabama School of Law. A dedicated proponent of law and order, at one point in time, Stephens had more prisoners sentenced to death row than any prosecutor in the state.

Stephens began his law career in private practice. In 1952, he was appointed district attorney for the 12th Judicial Circuit, following his predecessor Eris Paul's election as circuit judge. After serving in that position for five years, he returned to private practice. In 1965, he was again appointed district attorney. After completing the second interim term, he sought election in his own right and remained in the office until retiring in 1978.

An active member of the Alabama National Guard, Stephens steadily rose in rank over the course of 30 years of faithful duty. Even in the civilian world, some people addressed him as "Colonel Stephens." While he was never a particularly physically imposing figure, standing only about five-feet, seven-inches-tall, and a bit on the pudgy side, the silver-haired district attorney nonetheless appeared distinguished. Dale Marsh recalled Stephens most memorable feature was the "twinkle in his blue eyes." While generally easygoing, if Stephens grew angry, it was a corker.

Years later, Stephens' son, Daniel, remembered his father "loved his work" and "did not like to lose." As the father of five, the district attorney made it a point "not to bring his work home," where it might intrude on family time.

Stephens and Marsh grew closer while the two of them served in the National Guard. Eventually, Stephens invited the younger lawyer to join him as assistant district attorney. According to Marsh, Stephens was a good "plea dealer" who, at this point late in his career, had no misgivings about assigning the "more glamorous cases" to his young assistant, who was more than eager to gain the courtroom experience.

Born in the Goodman community, just west of Enterprise, Dale Marsh moved to town when he was in the fourth grade. After graduating from high school in 1966, he earned an undergraduate degree from Auburn University and then graduated from the University of Alabama School of Law. After returning to Enterprise in 1974, Marsh joined an established law firm anchored by Joe Cassidy, Sr. and Ken Fuller. In January of 1976, he would become a full partner in the firm. While expected to maintain a full private practice case load, Marsh took on the additional responsibilities of assistant district attorney in late 1976 or early 1977. At the time of the Hutto trial, he was a relative newcomer to the district attorney's office.

Six-feet, three-and-a-half-inches-tall and slender, Marsh was a notable presence in the courtroom. His dark black hair, blue eyes, direct manner, and booming yet melodic voice commanded attention from witnesses and jurors alike.

At that point in time, the county commission only paid the assistant district attorney a salary of $3,000 a year. Consequently, Marsh depended on fees generated from his private practice to supplement his income.

While working at a hectic pace in both the private and public sectors, Marsh recalled the upside: "The assistant district attorney's job gave an ambitious trial lawyer an early opportunity to gain valuable experience quickly. Many civil lawyers in big firms had to wait three to five years before being able to handle a case from start to top."

The defense team, Joe S. Pittman and Ken Hooks, would prove to be effective advocates for David Hutto. Born in Enterprise, Pittman attempted to join the military during World War II but was disqualified because of poor eyesight. He ultimately earned his undergraduate degree from Auburn University and started law school at Emory before transferring to the University of Alabama. Pittman, who was 53 years old, was well-known in the community, where he had practiced for nearly a quarter of a century. In the words of Dale Marsh, Pittman was "a county seat lawyer" who knew most of the town's citizens, kept close tabs on the words and actions of locals, maintained strong social and political connections, and was familiar with all the subtle nuances of trying a case on his home turf.

Pittman, who was five-feet, ten-inches-tall and of medium build, had slightly graying hair, which complemented his distinguished reputation. The classic small-town attorney, he practiced almost every kind of law, including civil, criminal, real estate, and tax cases. Judge Gary McAliley, who observed Pittman in action many times, remembered him as "a very good lawyer who was always prepared."

"He thoroughly defended his clients. A calculated and methodical thinker, he was also a gentleman who was respected by jurors," McAliley added.

Dale Marsh echoed McAliley's description of Pittman. Marsh also remembered Pittman was a skilled cross-examiner who could readily detect if witnesses were lying, contradicting themselves, or displaying obvious biases during their testimony.

Pittman spoke slowly and deliberately, a style that kept listeners, including jurors, hanging on his every word. At the same time, he was never one for small talk or gossip. Pittman was extremely protective of those who sought his representation.

He once told his nephew Don, now a practicing attorney in Enterprise: "The lawyer's greatest liability is not keeping his client's confidence."

Pittman's co-counsel, 26-year-old Ken Hooks, was born and raised in Orlando, Florida. A talented football player, he turned down athletic scholarships to focus on academics. After graduating high school in 1969, he attended Enterprise State Junior College, where he "got serious about school." He also became a skilled member of the debate team, which reinforced prior notions about his future.

"I knew, early on, I wanted to be a lawyer," Hooks recalled.

After junior college, Hooks transferred to the University of Alabama, where he completed his undergraduate and law degrees. Having passed the bar examination, Hooks joined Joe Pittman and Dick Whittaker at their established law firm in Enterprise. Athletically built at six-feet, two-inches-tall and weighing 190 pounds, Hooks had brown hair and piercing blue eyes.

His physicality was matched by ambition: "I was young and aggressive and wanted to be a trial lawyer."

In early January of 1977, Hooks was at the law firm's office on South Edwards Street when Hutto's wife and mother arrived unannounced to discuss legal representation for David. Lacking funds to hire a lawyer, the accused murderer would have to rely on representation by court-appointed attorneys. Although eager to take on the case, Hooks lacked the requisite number of years in practice to request a court appointment. Intrigued by Hutto's case, he approached Joe Pittman, who he considered "a man of great character" and convinced him the firm should represent the near-destitute defendant. In the end, the county paid the attorneys only $1,526, equating to what Hooks estimated as being roughly 50 cents an hour, to represent Hutto during both of his trials.

"It was essentially a pro bono case," Hooks said.

Hooks compensated for his youth with enthusiasm and legal acumen. Gary McAliley remembered Hooks was "brilliant and had a near-photographic memory." The former judge also noted both Hooks and Pittman readily did "just things" for their clients, including taking on a fair share of pro bono cases.

When the two attorneys agreed to represent Hutto, not everyone in town was happy. Because Pittman also served as Enterprise's city attorney, many police officers were less than pleased to learn he would be representing an accused murderer. Pittman, however, was non-plussed. In 1964, along with Elba attorney Garth Lindsay, he had taken on the unpopular court-appointed task of representing Ben Mathis, the man convicted of murdering Mr. and Mrs. Ed Morgan.

On January 10, 1977, Pittman, Hooks, and their third partner, Dick Whittaker, were formally appointed by Judge Riley Green to represent David Hutto. Whittaker, however, apparently never played an active role in the case. Already girded for battle, that same day, the defense team requested a bond hearing.

Three days later, *The Elba News* reported the court-appointed attorneys appeared before Judge Green to formally ask for a change of venue in Hutto's forthcoming murder trial. The defense team argued there was "so great a prejudice against the defendant that he cannot obtain a fair trial in Coffee County." Separate motions were also filed by the defense requesting the prosecution disclose all evidence against the defendant and for a hearing to "determine if Hutto was entitled to bond." That same day, Hutto made his first appearance in court since his indictment and arrest. The defendant informed Judge Green he could not afford to hire an attorney and was dependent on court-appointed representation. At this point, Judge Green apparently deferred rulings on the defense motions to the trial judge.

On Monday, January 17, 1977, Judge Terry Butts, who would be trying the case, held a bond hearing. The original bond had been fixed at $50,000 by Judge Green following Hutto's indictment and arrest. Joe Pittman argued the amount was exorbitant. He also pointed out Hutto was not a property owner, had a wife and two young children, and lived with his mother, whose only income came from her Social Security check.

"David's work and livelihood are derived from working in the building trade as a roofer, and that has necessitated his living day to day, week by week. We feel that this amount is tantamount to saying he is not permitted to have bond," Pittman implored.

The defense attorney also requested his client be allowed to testify. Pittman hoped "whatever he says will have some bearing on the situation and the amount of bond."

However, before Hutto took the stand, Pittman further clarified the record: "There have been rumors that David has been away and has been in the service (in the nine years since Buford Lolley was murdered), but all during this time, he has been in Enterprise, living there continuously."

The attorney added to his appeal, proclaiming Hutto "was a young boy, a teenager, and since then, he has married and taken on obligations as the head of a household and has been there working every day." Now on a roll, Pittman asserted Hutto had "fully and totally" cooperated with local and state investigators.

"He has cooperated with the authorities from the morning after this heinous crime took place, when the police fanned out in the community where David was then living. That reason alone seems to me to have some bearing on what bond should be set," Pittman explained.

Directing his gaze toward District Attorney Lewey L. Stephens, Jr., Pittman displayed a measure of indignation: "I have searched long and hard to try and find and satisfy my mind on what the state has against this young man now that they haven't had since the day after the crime. We haven't found anything."

Afterward, Hutto took the stand and answered a few questions from Pittman concerning his living arrangements and prior cooperation with law enforcement. The defendant explained that he lived in his mother's house at the time of Buford Lolley's murder, located a short distance from the Save-Way gas station. Hutto also recalled the police coming to the house on the morning of the murder and "off and on" in the days to follow.

District Attorney Stephens eventually objected to the nature of Pittman's questions. Consequently, the prosecution and defense lawyers met with Judge Butts in his chambers. The specific details of the conference were not reported to the press and cannot be recalled by any of the participants. However, when the group returned to the courtroom, Pittman announced he had no further questions and asked the judge to set the bail "as low as possible."

While presenting the state's argument against lowering the defendant's bail, Stephens pointed out that Hutto was a convicted felon, related to a grand larceny in Dale County, and had been previously convicted for escaping from a detention facility in Elmore County. Despite Pittman's impassioned appeals, round one of the arguments in the Lolley murder case was decided in favor of the prosecution. Consequently, Hutto would remain in jail until at least the conclusion of his first trial.

Early on, Ken Hooks concluded Hutto's defense "would not be a fair fight." At that point in time, the defense attorney recalled most juries were "hell bent on prosecution."

"Jurors were predisposed to believe that a person who was indicted was guilty. That was just the culture," Hooks remembered.

A veteran local jurist amplified Hooks' premise, agreeing that most juries were the "hanging kind," more likely than not to side with the prosecution. At first glance, Hutto's chances of being acquitted appeared to be slim.

Hooks recalled "there was absolutely no discovery from the prosecution," so other than "possibly" receiving a list of witnesses, the defense attorneys had no clear understanding about the strength of the state's case. When the defense team subsequently introduced motions to obtain evidence accumulated by the district attorney's office and asked for a change of venue, both were denied by Judge Butts.

Since Hutto had been indicted before he was arrested, a preliminary hearing was not mandated, at which time the defense lawyers might have learned at least skeletal details about the strength of the prosecution's case against their client. Hooks characterized this chain of events as "a tactical maneuver by the prosecution."

"We knew nothing; it was a trial by ambush," Hooks declared, without reservation.

Dale Marsh essentially agreed with Hooks' assessment, remembering there was no discovery in criminal trials at that point in time. He recalled the district attorney's office would sometimes indict a suspect before law enforcement made the arrest, thereby avoiding a preliminary hearing. Had there been a preliminary hearing for Hutto, Marsh is certain the state would have presented as little information as possible about its case. In retrospect, he was not even sure if the prosecution provided the defense with a witness list.

For the defense, there was always one constant. Throughout the pre-trial preparation, Hooks distinctly remembered his client "never moved an inch off his story." Hutto repeatedly informed his lawyers that he did not kill Buford Lolley and was truly perplexed about why he had been arrested and indicted for murder. Furthermore, the defendant never asked about the possibility of a plea deal.

Although Hooks was convinced that his client was not guilty, he did worry about Hutto's lazy eye, which resulted in involuntary and somewhat unusual facial expressions. Describing Hutto's countenance as sometimes "eerie," Hooks was concerned the jury would have "a hard time looking at him" when the defendant took the witness stand. In addition to being afflicted with strabismus, Hutto's courtroom attire lacked sartorial elegance.

"We had no money for David to spruce up for court," his wife said, "I don't know if the jail offered a haircut or not."

During one of the two trials, when David appeared for court dressed in a mismatched combination of red and white checkered pants and a blue shirt, Joe Pittman was concerned enough to ask his client if "he didn't have any better clothes to wear." Despite his inelegant wardrobe, Susan Hutto remembered her husband proudly "held his head up and went on about the court's day of business."

David Hutto's murder trial began at 9:00 a.m. on Monday, March 28, 1977. It was the first of 10 cases on the court's docket. Under sunny skies accompanied by mild temperatures and a slight breeze, 101 prospective jurors were summoned to the courthouse in Enterprise. The jury pool was questioned in mass by the lawyers and the judge. The judge began by granting excusals for reasons such as a prospective juror being related to the defendant or the victim, illiteracy, health problems, and physical disabilities. During voir dire, the prosecution and defense were given the same number of peremptory strikes, using them in alternate fashion until a panel of 12, seven men and five women, were qualified to sit in judgment of David Hutto.

In this particular case, no alternate jurors were selected. According to an attorney practicing in Enterprise at that time, decisions about whether or not to qualify alternate jurors were arbitrary and at the trial judge's discretion.

Judge Butts specifically recalled the qualification of alternate jurors was a rarity before the 1980s.

Judge Butts notified the jurors that they would be sequestered at a local motel for the duration of the trial. Most likely, the jurors stayed at the Enterpriser Motel on the southern end of the bypass. (The full traffic circle had not yet been constructed.) There were only three such lodgings in town, and the other two, the Averett Motel and the Terry Motel, had seen better days.

The judge informed the panel of their responsibility to render a verdict in the murder trial. He also explained that if the defendant was found guilty, it would be up to the jury to decide his punishment.

As the trial unfolded, *The Daily Ledger* reported ongoing tension between the family and friends of Buford Lolley and those who supported David Hutto. However, for the duration of the trial, there were no demonstrations or outbursts from the gallery.

As might have been expected in such a high-profile case, the courtroom was packed, including a number of students from a local junior high school civics class, who were allowed to attend the trial and learn firsthand about the judicial process. On the third day of the trial, Judge Butts did order some of the students to be removed from the courtroom to ease overcrowding. Even during the late stages of the trial, while the jury was undertaking lengthy deliberations, the courtroom gallery remained close to half full.

At 2:00 p.m., after jury selection and opening statements by the attorneys on both sides, the state began presenting its case against Hutto. The contents of the opening statements were not recorded by the press. According to Dale Marsh, opening statements were very brief, usually not more than five to 10 minutes long. Both sides simply introduced themselves and informed the jury what they intended to prove, without going into any specific details.

On Monday afternoon, the prosecution proceeded to call five witnesses to the stand. The first witness, Junior Farris, a former Enterprise Police Department Corporal who had been in charge of coordinating shifts, was questioned by District Attorney Stephens. Farris explained he was on patrol in the early-morning hours of January 14, 1968, keeping a watchful eye on the security of local businesses and residences.

Farris testified he drove past the Save-Way gas station at 3:15 a.m. and saw Buford Lolley standing just inside the building. The overnight attendant was very much alive, taking time to wave at the passing patrol car. Farris recalled that the area was well lit, and he did not notice any other people in the vicinity of the station. To ensure that Farris possessed the ability to recognize the gas station attendant, the district attorney questioned the former policeman about his familiarity with Lolley. Farris testified he had known him for "around seven or eight years."

At 3:39 a.m., only 24 minutes after he had seen Lolley alive, Farris received an urgent message over his police radio about the murder, according to his testimony. When he arrived at the Save-Way, Officers McDaniel and Tidwell were at the scene of the crime. The police chief and county sheriff soon arrived at the gas station.

Because of the lack of a trial transcript, the chronology and actual testimony offered during Hutto's trials have been reconstructed from newspaper coverage and 44-year-old individual and collective memories from people who were in the courtroom. According to these sources, either defense attorney Joe Pittman did not question Farris, or the content of his cross-examination was unremarkable.

Enterprise Police Department Lieutenant J.B. McDaniel was the second witness called by the prosecution. Under direct examination, he testified that he and his partner, Officer Tidwell, had driven by the Save-Way station at approximately 3:00 a.m. on the day of Lolley's murder. While passing by the station, McDaniel clearly saw Lolley, who was sitting in a chair inside the building, according to his testimony.

When the police officers stopped at the Save-Way at 3:39 a.m., McDaniel discovered glass on the floor of the gas station and a trail of blood leading from the front door to Lolley's body. McDaniel noted the attendant was lying on the floor, with blood still flowing from the wounds on his head and arm.

When Stephens questioned the witness about his subsequent actions, McDaniel testified he and Tidwell secured the area and did not disturb the evidence until Chief Murdock arrived at the scene of the crime. According to McDaniel, the chief of police was the second person to enter the building.

The district attorney proceeded to ask McDaniel about the location of Lolley's body. The police lieutenant testified the decedent was lying on his back with his head facing southward. Testifying about the condition of the body, McDaniel grimly recalled part of Lolley's head had been "knocked off."

On cross-examination, Joe Pittman once again had McDaniel describe the murder scene. His testimony was essentially the same, with a few additional observations. The police lieutenant reported blood was spattered on the inside walls of the station, and it appeared Lolley had been bludgeoned "numerous times." McDaniel also believed Lolley had been dead for only a few minutes because blood was still flowing from his body. After further questioning, McDaniel provided jurors with a brief description of the decedent's body habitus: medium height and somewhat overweight.

Enterprise Police Chief Howard Murdock was the third prosecution witness to take the stand. It soon appeared he had neither reviewed the case file nor seriously rehearsed his testimony. On direct examination, the police chief recalled being summoned to the murder scene by Lieutenant McDaniel, who had discovered Lolley's battered body. Murdock also remembered encountering the corpse in the "right corner" of the gas station accompanied by "quite a bit of blood on the floor beside him." However, when the district attorney asked the most basic of questions, whether any money was stolen from the gas station at the time of the murder, Murdock testified he could not remember and "would hesitate to say."

Even though he may have been stunned by Murdock's major memory lapse, Stephens did not break stride, asking the police chief if he was familiar with State Toxicologist Guy Purnell. Murdock testified he did not know the toxicologist but did accompany him to Searcy Funeral Home, where Purnell performed an autopsy on Lolley's body. At this point, perhaps wisely so, the prosecution ended its direct examination of the witness.

On cross-examination, Pittman asked Murdock various questions about the murder scene. The police chief testified Lolley had been beaten with a heavy metal object, and one of the gas station's side doors had been damaged by an errant blow from the murder weapon.

"The room was very bloody, and there was a trail of blood leading to the front door," Murdock explained.

When asked if the blood appeared to be smudged, the chief did not recall any distortion of the blood trail. The cross-examination of Murdock continued and would prove to be the lengthiest and most detailed testimony of the day.

Probing another area of the investigation, Pittman asked the police chief if he remembered going to David Hutto's mother's home at approximately

7:30 on the morning of the murder, where he discovered the defendant was still asleep. While uncertain about the time, Murdock remembered Hutto was at home and asleep. The defense attorney then asked if Hutto's clothing and shoes were examined for blood stains. Murdock indirectly answered in the negative, indicating Hutto "was not a real suspect."

Pittman proceeded to ask a series of questions about whether the police chief questioned Hutto about his whereabouts at the time of the murder and when he returned home on the night of January 13–14. While Murdock could not recall if he asked Hutto where he was when Lolley was murdered, the chief remembered the defendant told him he returned home between 12:30 a.m. and 1:00 a.m. Not yet done, Murdock added "that in his experience as a law officer, he did not always accept as truth statements made by suspects."

Had Murdock's conflicting statements escaped the jury? At first, the chief of police testified Hutto *was not* a suspect but then implied the defendant *was* a suspect. Those contradictions must have been quite evident to the defense team.

Pittman continued his cross-examination of Murdock, asking if the chief returned to Hutto's home about a week after the murder to once again question David about his whereabouts at the time of Lolley's murder. Murdock had no memory of any return visit.

When the defense attorney asked Murdock if he recalled accompanying a state investigator and two suspects to Montgomery, the chief answered affirmatively. After reminding Murdock that the unidentified suspects had been interviewed for two hours, Pittman asked him if he regarded the state law enforcement officer as a "competent investigator." Murdock refused to offer an opinion about the investigator's competency but recalled "there had been some conflicting information brought into the case." There is no record, however, of Murdock clarifying the nature of the so-called "conflicting information."

When Pittman asked if the interviews of those two suspects led to investigations of other individuals potentially connected to the murder, Murdock answered yes. The defense attorney then asked the chief to identify those additional suspects. Murdock responded by reading aloud a list of some *eight* to *10* people and indicated there might be others he had not named. Without explanation, the names of those individuals were never reported by *The Daily Ledger*. Years later, Dale Marsh speculated that David Hutto,

Billy Wayne Bradley, and Odell Belcher were among the names recited by the police chief.

Pittman proceeded to ask Murdock if he was aware that a state investigator later interviewed one of the suspects who had moved to Maryland. After testifying neither he nor any member of the Enterprise Police Department interviewed the man in question, Murdock acknowledged the state lawman had interrogated the suspect. When the defense attorney identified the suspect as Jim Castle, Murdock verified the name and testified that Castle was married to David Hutto's sister. According to the chief, Castle was living in Enterprise at the time of Lolley's murder, about a mile from the Save-Way station. Though not mentioned by the press, Castle's interrogation apparently shed no new light on the case.

The defense attorney then asked the police chief if he had interviewed two people who lived on Erin Street, just across South Main Street from the gas station, about what they saw and heard around the time of the murder. Murdock admitted to having spoken with "a Sergeant Kellum and his wife." The witnesses Pittman was referring to were the mysterious Mr. and Mrs. X mentioned in the 1975 newspaper articles that re-examined the murder.

Shifting gears, Pittman asked Murdock if he recalled conducting a press conference shortly after Lolley's murder, at which time he described the coats worn by two suspects seen leaving the gas station around the time of murder, based on information provided by the couple living on Erin Street. The chief answered yes.

Pittman then inquired if Murdock recalled telling David Hutto's mother that her son did not murder Buford Lolley. The chief testified he "might have made statements to that effect, but only to calm the woman, who was old and very worried about her son." In this case, age must have been in the eye of the beholder because Inez Hutto was only 57 years old in 1968. Murdock explained his previous testimony in a confusing manner, indicating the statement about Hutto not being the killer "did not mean that was the right conclusion."

For now, Pittman kept Murdock focused on his visit to Hutto's mother's house on the morning of the murder. When asked if he went there to search for "blood stains or blood on the clothes," Murdock replied that he was "making a survey." Questioned about whether the murderer "would have to have been covered with blood from the physical appearance at the scene of the killing," the police chief opined the killer would "mostly likely would have had blood on them."

Under further questioning, Chief Murdock testified that the police "never found any blood on the clothes at the Hutto house, nor his shoes." With this initial sworn statement about examining Hutto's clothing, the police chief initiated what would become a controversial issue concerning the police department's investigation.

When asked about fingerprint testing, the chief replied: "We checked to the best of our ability for fingerprints."

Pittman then read aloud a statement reporting that no fingerprints had been discovered at the Huttos' house. In response, Murdock acknowledged that was true.

When Pittman proceeded to ask if Hutto had been taken to Montgomery to take a lie detector test, District Attorney Stephens interrupted, reminding Judge Butts the entire line of questioning about polygraph testing originated from the defense rather than the prosecution. At this point, Butts apparently overruled the initial objection related to questions about the use of polygraphs. After postulating that Hutto passed the lie detector test, Pittman asked Murdock if he informed David's mother that her son was "not involved in the crime."

After the prosecution once again objected, Judge Butts ordered the jury removed from the courtroom before declaring "there was no law in the state to my knowledge which allowed for the admission of polygraph test results as admission of evidence in a trial." Consequently, Butts ruled he would not allow any further testimony regarding that subject. The defense was forced to accept Butts' ruling. Pittman, however, "protested" that the state had not made any polygraph test results available to Hutto's lawyers.

Nearing the end of his cross-examination of Murdock, Pittman asked who was present at the Huttos' home when the police chief visited on the morning of January 14, 1968. Murdock recalled David Hutto, his mother, possibly one of David's sisters, and some small children were inside the house.

In closing, Pittman asked Murdock if he observed any washed clothes at Hutto's residence. The chief answered yes, adding David's mother verified she had washed clothes very early that morning. When asked if those clothes had been inspected, Murdock answered in the negative. Earlier, however, Murdock testified there was *no blood* found on Hutto's clothes or shoes.

Consequently, it remains unknown if the police chief ever examined any of Hutto's wardrobe, washed or unwashed.

After Pittman concluded his thorough cross-examination of Murdock, it was obvious the Enterprise police chief had been anything but a strong witness for the prosecution. Many portions of his testimony had been vague, uncertain, and contradictory.

The prosecution's fourth witness, Guy Purnell, was a former Alabama state toxicologist who had since moved to Philadelphia. Purnell testified that he drove from Montgomery to Enterprise on the morning of Buford Lolley's murder. After arriving in Enterprise, Purnell joined State Investigator J.R. Pate in coordinating the investigation. Accompanied by Pate and Chief Murdock, Purnell traveled to Searcy Funeral Home and performed an autopsy on Lolley. The toxicologist, however, could not recall if Pate and Murdock were actually present in the room when he was conducting the autopsy.

After Purnell provided a detailed description of the decedent's wounds, District Attorney Stephens asked the toxicologist if he formulated an opinion as to how many times Lolley had been struck. Purnell counted "at least seven wounds," including one that "penetrated the brain cavity." Purnell further testified the cause of death was a direct result of blows on the head with "some sort of heavy blunt instrument."

"That is still my opinion," he emphasized.

While at the crime scene, Purnell had discovered the 13-inch-long steel weapon on top of the laundry across the street from the Save-Way gas station, according to his testimony. Using an adjacent fence to gain access to the roof, the toxicologist located the weapon "almost immediately."

Purnell reported that the blood and hair discovered on the weapon and analyzed by crime lab technicians matched the murder victim. He also recalled seeing an "indentation" on the inside of the gas station's side door, consistent with an errant blow from the murder weapon.

Since Purnell proved to be a solid prosecution witness, his cross-examination was brief. When Pittman asked the toxicologist how much physical strength would have been necessary to kill Lolley using such a weapon, Purnell declined to offer an opinion. The defense attorney also asked Purnell if he received a letter containing a two-dollar bill on January 31, 1968, accompanied by a note requesting the paper money be tested for blood. The toxicologist responded in the affirmative, before testifying that laboratory studies revealed no traces of blood on the currency.

The testimony about the two-dollar bill may have raised more than one question in jurors' minds. Was it the same two-dollar bill Lolley kept in his wallet, or was it a hoax? If it had belonged to the murder victim, who had sent the currency to state investigators? Had one of the robbers eventually developed some semblance of remorse?

The fifth and final prosecution witness of the day was Mary Lipford, *The Daily Ledger's* previously unidentified Mrs. X. Assistant District Attorney Marsh started his questioning by exploring her background. Lipford testified she was living with her now ex-husband Fred W. Kellum at the time of Lolley's murder. In January of 1968, the couple lived in a rental house at 201 Erin Street, just across South Main Street from the Save-Way gas station, she said.

Marsh showed Lipford several photographs of her former residence and its proximity to the gas station and a well-lit used car lot also located across the street. The defense immediately objected to the pictures being offered into evidence, not knowing when and where the photographs were taken. After Marsh informed the judge that the photos were taken by Roy Shoffner, the editor of *The Daily Ledger*, Butts overruled the objection and allowed the pictures to be entered into evidence.

After further questioning by the prosecution, Mrs. Lipford said that both she and her then-husband heard an unusual noise in the early-morning hours of January 14, 1968. At first, she thought "it was cats fighting." Afterward, the couple looked out their bedroom window toward the Save-Way and saw "two boys" at the gas station.

At this point, inconsistencies in Mary Lipford's and Fred Kellum's past statements compared to their trial testimony first became apparent. Sergeant Kellum never made mention of *seeing anyone* when he was interviewed by *The Daily Ledger* in 1975. In addition, Lipford told the newspaper reporter she did not see the youths until peering outside the bedroom window a *second* time.

As her direct testimony proceeded, Lipford testified that one of the two boys was outside the station door, and the other was still inside the building in a bent-over position. This portion of her testimony was different from what was recorded in the 1975 newspaper article, at which time Mrs. X stated the first suspect was the one who was in a bent-over position. Eventually, the youth inside the station joined his partner, and the pair crossed South Main Street, "walking fast but not running," and headed in the general direction of the Kellum's house.

When Marsh asked about visibility on that early morning, Lipford reiterated that the area was well-lit by the used car lot across the street from their house. She then testified one suspect was wearing a "light topcoat" while the other was clad in a "fleece-lined jacket." After her then-husband concluded that the prior commotion most likely originated from two kids "cutting the fool with the man at the gas station," the couple returned to bed.

Lipford testified she first learned about Lolley's murder at around noon on January 14th and immediately notified local law enforcement officers about what she had observed in the early-morning hours. She also recalled visiting the Enterprise Police Department "off and on" for two weeks after the murder, reviewing mug shots and trying to positively identify the two suspects. She also provided details that helped the police draw composite sketches of the two suspects. Lipford later testified that the couple moved from Erin Street in February, just a month after Lolley's murder, "because we were kind of frightened."

Lipford's testimony had been solid, and Joe Pittman's cross-examination was brief. The witness confirmed that she had assisted the police in drawing composite pictures of the suspects. The defense attorney then asked how much time elapsed from the time Lipford moved from Erin Street in February of 1968 until law enforcement officers once again reached out to her. She testified that State Investigator J.R. Pate contacted her in late 1973 or early 1974 and that there was no further contact with state law enforcement until ABI Investigator Steve Weekley interviewed her in 1976, the same year that David Hutto was arrested.

Sometime after 5:00 p.m., Judge Butts halted testimony in day one of the trial. After instructing the jurors not to engage in conversations "regarding any aspect of the trial," he ordered them to be sequestered at the motel until court resumed at 8:30 the following morning.

On Tuesday morning, Police Chief Howard Murdock was recalled to the witness stand by the defense. The reason for the disruption in the flow of testimony is not entirely clear, but it appears the defense may have reserved the right to reexamine the police chief if any additional evidence was uncovered before court reconvened, information that could weaken his credibility as witness. Defense attorney Joe Pittman was certainly primed for additional cross-examination.

Pittman promptly asked Murdock if he ever made the statement: "David Hutto did not kill Buford Lolley but that he knew who did."

District Attorney Stephens immediately objected, asserting the defense was not following "the rules set forth for the basis of questioning." Pittman countered that his client was "on trial for his life" and the defense was entitled by law to a "wide range" during cross-examination. Stephens argued that Pittman's questions had to be more specific regarding when and where Murdock might have made any such statements. Judge Butts' ruling on the state's objection was not recorded by newspaper reporters. However, when Pittman resumed his cross-examination, the question remained essentially the same.

He proceeded to ask Murdock if he ever stated: "You did not believe David Hutto killed Buford Lolley but that he knew who did."

The police chief admitted he had done so on *one* unspecified occasion. The defense attorney tried to narrow down the time by asking Murdock if he uttered those words after Hutto's grand jury indictment. Murdock answered no, testifying he had "not been around the defendant" since his indictment. In reality, the chief of police had seen Hutto *at least once* while the defendant was incarcerated at the county jail in Elba following his indictment and arrest.

The defense continued to follow the same line of questioning. Pittman was determined to learn more precisely when and where the chief of police stated he thought Hutto was innocent of murder.

District Attorney Stephens immediately objected: "The question is too general in covering an eight- or nine-year span of time."

After Judge Butts overruled the state's objection, Pittman dug deeper, asking Murdock if he told Hutto's sister Frances Jenkins, while transporting her to the county jail to visit her brother, that he did not believe David killed Buford Lolley. Murdock testified he could not precisely recall but *may have said* that to Jenkins, hoping his statement would convince Hutto to reveal additional information about the Lolley murder. The police chief theorized that if Hutto was at scene of the crime but did not commit murder, he "must know who did."

Once again, Stephens objected, arguing Pittman was engaging in argumentative questioning. This time, Judge Butts sustained the objection.

However, Pittman was relentless. He once again asked Murdock if he made a statement suggesting David Hutto was innocent of murder after the defendant's indictment less than four months ago. This time, the police chief answered *yes*, yet another contradiction from his earlier testimony.

Not satisfied that the witness had been fully forthcoming, Pittman asked the chief if he ever made that same statement to Hutto's mother. Murdock testified he "could not give a definite yes or no without qualifying the answer by saying that he might have, in an effort to fish more information from the suspect." When asked if he was still "fishing" for information, Murdock answered no.

Shifting gears, Pittman asked the police chief if he had ever seen Hutto wearing the same type of coat Mary Lipford had described in her testimony. Murdock promptly answered yes.

"Did you search for that coat on the morning of the 14th when you went to his house?" Pittman inquired.

The police chief said he did not because he lacked a search warrant. Pittman then asked if the Hutto family had not "volunteered any and all cooperation" in the absence of a search warrant. Again, Murdock answered in the affirmative, adding Hutto "had always cooperated."

The jurors were left to ponder at what point Chief Murdock had observed Hutto wearing a brown fleece-lined jacket. In addition, the chief did not satisfactorily explain why he failed conduct a more thorough search of the Huttos' house, especially after the family volunteered to cooperate without a warrant,

In his final question, Pittman hoped Murdock would validate one of the defense team's primary theories, asking Murdock if it had been his intention all along to "indict the weakest link in the chain," forcing Hutto to disclose the name of the real killer. Before the police chief could respond, Stephens forcefully objected, asserting the chief of police had no say in who was indicted, a decision made exclusively by the district attorney's office.

Pittman had no further questions, but the damage had been done. Even though he was the chief of the Enterprise Police Department, Murdock's testimony during the second round of cross-examination revealed a number of inconsistencies and failed to bolster the state's case.

The prosecution's next witness was Sergeant Fred W. Kellum, who had been referred to as Mr. X in the 1975 media re-examination of the Lolley cold case. A US Army soldier now stationed in Germany, he had been flown back to Alabama by the state to testify.

The now ex-husband of Mary Lipford, Kellum recalled that early on the morning Buford Lolley was murdered, the couple had heard a strange noise coming from the vicinity of the Save-Way gas station across the street from their rental home. Kellum testified that he heard someone "calling for help." His wife then looked out their bedroom window and saw "two boys" crossing South Main Street as they were leaving the gas station. Kellum also testified that his wife had concluded the commotion "was kids cutting the fool." While not of major significance, Mary Lipford had earlier testified that it was Kellum who had made the "cutting the fool" comment.

His most damaging testimony soon followed. Kellum testified that after he went to the kitchen to get a drink of water, he looked out the window facing Erin Street and saw two young men pass directly in front of him. Kellum later identified one of them as David Hutto, based on a "three-quarter facial view" of the subject at a distance of only three feet. However, during the 1975 media blitz, Mr. X told reporters he had *seen no one* while looking through *any* of the house's windows.

On cross-examination, Joe Pittman immediately confronted the prosecution's witness. The defense attorney wanted to know why Kellum had not shared his identification of Hutto with local and state law enforcement officers immediately after the murder. Kellum explained that, at the time, he was "fearful for his life and for the lives of his family."

Seemingly unconvinced, Pittman asked Kellum why he allowed his wife to cooperate with police "almost daily" for two weeks after the murder. The witness explained his wife *did not know* he had seen one of the suspects clearly enough to identify him. Since his wife could only "partially identify clothing," Kellum concluded she was safe from any form of violent retaliation by Lolley's murderer.

As the cross-examination progressed, Kellum testified that he *first* revealed his identification of David Hutto as a suspect after his ex-wife wrote him and requested he get in touch with ABI Investigator Steve Weekley. When interviewed by Weekley in the summer of 1976, Kellum told the investigator he *could identify* the man he had seen outside his kitchen window. He also informed Weekley he was willing to return to the United States and testify against Hutto "since he had remarried, and his family was safe."

After Kellum was provided a copy of the written statement he made to Alabama State Investigator B.J. Gatlin in 1968, Pittman asked the witness to read it aloud. The content of the statement was consistent with Kellum's earlier court testimony, minus his highly incriminating identification of David Hutto as a suspect in the murder of Buford Lolley.

Pittman then asked Kellum if the prosecution or anyone else had discussed the possibility of a monetary reward with him. While the witness admitted his wife had mentioned the reward in her letter to him, Kellum stated the prosecutors guaranteed him nothing more than reimbursement for airfare and other expenses related to his return from Germany to testify.

At this point, the defense attorney proceeded to adopt a more accusatory tone with the witness. After he was specifically questioned, Kellum testified he actually met David Hutto *after* Lolley's murder, when he sold the defendant an automobile. Pittman further inquired if Investigator Weekley had contacted Kellum in Europe and indicated he would like for him to "hang David Hutto." The prosecution vehemently objected, accusing the defense of trying to "hang this witness."

"He needs to be hanged!" Pittman retorted.

Judge Butts immediately intervened, warning the lawyers to refrain from further use of any such language. He also instructed the jury to disregard previous statements related to "hanging."

Concluding his cross-examination, Pittman asked Kellum if he had sold Hutto a car and "on occasion, mingled socially with him, drinking a beer." The witness denied there had been any social mingling but verified he sold Hutto an automobile and testified he *might* have had a beer with the defendant outside his house. This interaction between Kellum and Hutto occurred after Lolley's murder. With the passage of time, could Kellum have been confused as to when and where he first saw Hutto's face?

Neither Lipford nor Kellum testified about seeing either suspect tossing an object on the roof of the Enterprise Laundry. However, during the 1975 media reinvestigation of Lolley's murder, Terry Everett wrote in *The Daily Ledger* that one of the suspects had discarded what was likely the murder weapon on the roof of the building. It is not known if some unknown person witnessed this action or if it was an assumption based on where the weapon was eventually located.

The next witness called by the prosecution offered perhaps the most damaging testimony against David Hutto. Thirty-five-year-old Patsy Hanks was controversial from the beginning. An attorney who was present at the trial and also quite familiar with Hanks later recalled that "she came up hard," "was poorly educated," "wore a lot of make-up," and dressed rather provocatively during her court appearances. It is quite possible Hanks' less-than-stellar reputation in the community and her manner of dress may have alienated some of the more conservative jurors. This same attorney also believed Hanks, who was not unattractive, had a "crush" on the handsome and clean-cut ABI Investigator Steve Weekley, who she frequently addressed as "Weeks." A long-time resident of Enterprise, who by reputation rarely criticizes others, did not mince words when describing Hanks as a "floozie." However, if the jury believed Hank's testimony, she would serve as a crucial witness for the state.

Hanks began her testimony by recalling October of 1968, when she was separated from her husband and living with Gladys Warren in Enterprise. Warren was apparently one of Hanks' friends or at least a close acquaintance. That same month, an "alcohol and pot party" was held at Warrens' house, just eight months after Buford Lolley was murdered. Hanks testified that during the course of the party, she had overhead David Hutto, whom she had known "since he was eight years old," indicate he was present at the Save-Way gas station when Buford Lolley was murdered but that he had not been the one who killed him. She also recalled Hutto identifying Billy Wayne Bradley as the actual murderer. According to Hanks, Hutto informed other party attendees that Bradley killed Lolley "only because he woke up from sleep."

When the prosecution asked Hanks if Hutto mentioned the instrument used to bludgeon Lolley to death, she remembered him stating Bradley was angry about "the weapon being thrown on top of the dry-cleaning building." Hanks further testified that Hutto informed others about the police picking up a young man named Gene Thomas to question him about Lolley's murder. The authorities apparently tried to intimidate Thomas by showing him photographs of the gas station attendant's body. According to Hanks, Hutto laughed because Thomas "had broken up over the picture."

Hanks also testified that Hutto had bragged "the pigs would never find out who killed Buford Lolley and which way they went."

The longer Hanks testified, the more she incriminated Hutto. While at the party, she had overheard Hutto confess to burning his blood-stained clothes in the fireplace at his mother's house on the morning of the murder.

Hanks also said that on January 13, 1968, one day before Buford Lolley was murdered, she was at the VPW Club in Samson, 25 miles southwest of Enterprise. While at the club, she saw her brother, Billy Ray Myers, talking with David Hutto and Billy Wayne Bradley. She recalled Hutto and Bradley asking her brother to return to Enterprise with them, but Myers declined the invitation. Since Hanks' brother was not particularly well-regarded in the community and would later become a convicted felon, it appears the state wanted to prove that Hutto associated with individuals whose reputations were unsavory.

Nearing the end of her direct examination, Hanks testified that she did not immediately inform the police about the incriminating statements Hutto made during the party at Gladys Warren's house because she was "scared." She also remembered having encountered Hutto "on numerous occasions" since October of 1968 and neither "mentioned the conversation" she allegedly overheard at the party. Hanks said she first shared Hutto's damaging statements with ABI Investigator Steve Weekley after the lawman suggested they meet in nearby Dothan for a confidential interview. Narrowing the time frame, this interview would have occurred at some point between 1974, when Weekley became an ABI investigator, and December 13, 1976, when Hutto was arrested.

During cross-examination, the defense asked Hanks if the district attorney's office or Investigator Weekley had "promised her consideration" on behalf of her brother, Billy Ray Myers, who at the time was incarcerated in Dale County and awaiting trial on additional felony charges, in exchange for her testimony implicating David Hutto in the Lolley murder. Hanks denied receiving any "promises" from either the prosecution team or Weekley. Hanks did vow that "if she could find any evidence" that her brother was falsely convicted during a prior trial held in Coffee County, she would take it to the district attorney's office and "would expect a follow-through with the information."

Hanks admitted "after she fingered David Hutto for the police" that she visited him at one of his roofing work sites. At that time, Hanks informed Hutto she had implicated him in the Lolley murder, hoping he would go to the police himself. To the best of her knowledge, Hutto never contacted law enforcement authorities. Susan Hutto, however, has no recollection of Hanks visiting her husband while he was at work, but thinks it is possible that Hanks or one of her brothers met with David at a different location to let him know what she had told Investigator Weekley.

Hanks testified she had been threatened after informing Investigator Weekley about Hutto's alleged confession at the 1968 party. She specifically recalled being awakened in the middle of the night at her house in neighboring Ozark, terrified to discover a man's hand covering her mouth and a gun pointed at her head. The intruder warned her, in no uncertain terms, to never again speak with the police about either David Hutto or Billy Wayne Bradley. Because her bedroom was dark, Hanks could not positively identify the intruder but suspected it was David Hutto, Billy Wayne Bradley, or Hutto's brother.

While the defense no doubt questioned the veracity of Hanks' testimony, Joe Pittman maintained a gentlemanly tone, one that today might be considered patronizing. Instead of using her last name, Pittman addressed the witness as "Ms. Patsy." Under cross-examination, Hanks refused to back away from any of her direct testimony and denied she was being monetarily rewarded for appearing in court.

By the time she left the witness stand, Hanks had offered damaging testimony against Hutto. The jurors, however, were left to judge the truthfulness and reliability of her statements given under oath. Hanks' testimony also marked the end of the prosecution's case.

Joe Pittman and Ken Hooks were now responsible for presenting the defense's case. The two attorneys ultimately called several witnesses to the stand, with most of their testimonies being relatively brief.

Frances Jerkins, David Hutto's sister, was the first defense witness. Jerkins testified that she rode from Enterprise to the county jail in Elba in a car driven by Police Chief Murdock after her brother was indicted and arrested for murder. During the short trip, Jerkins recalled the police chief stating he did not believe Hutto killed Buford Lolley but "he knew who did." However, when Murdock repeated that statement in front of both Jerkins and her brother at the jail, David informed the chief "he did not commit the crime and did not know anybody who did." Jerkins' testimony indicated Murdock made that same statement *more than one time* and to *more than just one person*, directly contradicting the police chief's prior testimony.

Jerkins also testified that her brother never owned a brown fleece-lined coat as reported by some witnesses. In 1968, she recalled him possessing only blue, yellow, and green windbreakers. Any cross-examination of Jerkins by the state went unreported in the newspapers and is not recalled by trial participants or observers.

Twenty-eight-year-old James Miley Simmons soon took the stand. According to Patsy Hanks, Simmons had been present at the "beer and pot party" hosted by Gladys Warren in October of 1968. Simmons, however, testified he had visited Gladys Warren's only once and had never been in the presence of David Hutto and Patsy Hanks at the same time. Moreover, he denied knowing Patsy Hanks. Simmons also informed the jurors he never heard Hutto make any statements about Buford Lolley's murder. Simmons further testified he did not know Billy Wayne Bradley and never heard Hutto accuse Bradley of murdering Lolley.

Pittman asked Simmons if his brother, Gary, who had been subpoenaed as a witness but failed to show up for the trial, would also deny being present at the party where Hutto allegedly incriminated himself. District Attorney Stephens immediately objected to hearsay testimony. Stephens' objection was apparently sustained.

During a brief cross-examination, the prosecution called into question Simmons' character, which might cast doubt about his veracity, at least in the eyes of some jurors. When asked if he had been convicted of second-degree burglary, Simmons answered in the affirmative. Did a prior burglary conviction also make him a perjurer? In the final analysis, the jury was left to decide whether to give Simmons' or Hanks' testimony more weight.

The defense subsequently called Patsy Hanks' sister, Judy Grant, to the witness stand. Grant testified that ABI Investigator Weekley and a Dale County sheriff's deputy had come to her sister's house in Ozark to serve Hanks with a subpoena to testify in the Hutto murder trial. At the time, Grant testified Hanks was not at home. Grant, however, was under the impression both lawmen thought her sister was actually present in house but hiding from them.

"They said if my sister didn't come to the jail and get the subpoena today, we would never get to see our brother again, even on Sundays," Grant testified.

At this point in time, Hanks' and Grant's brother, Billy Ray Myers, was incarcerated in the Daily County jail, having already been convicted in Coffee County on two counts of rape and cleared on one case of kidnapping. In Dale County, Myers was awaiting trial on charges of kidnapping and car theft.

During cross-examination, Assistant District Attorney Marsh wanted to make it clear that neither the district attorney's office nor the ABI had threatened Pasty Hanks. After being questioned, Grant testified it was the deputy sheriff and not Weekley who threatened loss of visitation rights with their brother. She also admitted no one in law enforcement had prevented the family from seeing Myers, despite the deputy sheriff's previous warning.

Twenty-seven-year-old Jimmy Myers, another of Patsy Hanks' brothers, was the next defense witness. He testified that "Weekley threatened to beat the hell out of me" if Myers tried to keep Hanks from testifying in Hutto's murder trial.

Myers further testified that his sister, Patsy, would not tell the truth under oath and had a reputation for exaggerating. Myers also claimed Investigator Weekley told him that without Patsy Hanks' testimony, the prosecution "would not have a case." Myers admitted he tried to convince his sister not to testify, in large part because he refused to believe anything she said.

Under cross-examination by Marsh, Jimmy Myers seemed to be more focused on keeping his sister from aiding the prosecution than on her veracity. Myers testified he "hated the state" and would never do anything to help "the state of Alabama" because of his brother's prior arrests and convictions. His anger mounting, Myers proclaimed he would not assist the state even if he was an "eye-witness to a crime."

Marsh then asked Myers if he tried to scare or threaten Patsy to keep her from testifying for the state in this trial. While Myers replied he would do "anything in my power to keep her from testifying," he denied having scared or threatened his sister.

"Did you call her on the telephone and tell her that her car was going to be bombed?" Marsh asked.

"I did not," Myers replied, ending his cross-examination.

Anger clearly clouded Myers' judgment while he was under oath. Given his open disdain for law enforcement, it was difficult to know how much he actually discredited his sister as a truthful witness.

When 42-year-old Huey Thames took the stand, he testified that David Hutto left a pool room in Enterprise with him the day before Buford Lolley's murder and that the pair drove to a club in Florida. Between 7:00 p.m. and 8:00 p.m., the two of them decided to leave the club and head home, Thames recalled. During the return trip, Thames and Hutto stopped at Batten's Crossroads, just south of Enterprise, after encountering a stalled car. Thames remembered picking up the three stranded motorists: Billy Wayne Bradley, Billy Ray Myers, and another man he did not know. After returning to Enterprise to purchase gas, the entire group traveled to a dance in Samson.

Hutto and Thames, however, did not stay at the dance, instead returning to a pool hall in Enterprise. Thames testified he last saw Hutto late on the evening of January 13, 1968, when the pool hall was closing, just hours before Lolley was murdered.

Under Marsh's cross-examination, Thames direct testimony proved contradictory. He told the jury that he was not entirely sure the earlier events occurred on January 13th and could have occurred a *week* or even a *year* earlier. Thames also modified his earlier story, testifying that he and Hutto left Samson and drove back to the club in Florida to search for his lost wallet before returning to Enterprise. At the end of cross-examination, Thames' confusing testimony did little to clarify Hutto's whereabouts in the hours leading up to Lolley's murder.

The next defense witness, Ozark Police Department Investigator John Nicholson, was subpoenaed to offer testimony concerning Patsy Hanks's complaints of being threatened after she informed ABI Investigator Weekley about Hutto's incriminating statements concerning the Lolley murder. Nicholson reported that Hanks had filed three separate complaints about being threatened. If Nicholson revealed any details about his investigation of Hanks' complaints, they were not recorded by the press. However, since Nicholson was a defense witness, it is quite possible he discounted the severity of Hank's threats. Consequently, the jury was left to judge whether those threats were genuine, false, or manifestations of confused hysteria. There is no record of the prosecution cross-examining Nicholson.

David Hutto's brother, Billy, was called to the witness stand by the defense. During a brief direct examination, Billy denied threatening Patsy Hanks and testified that he did not even know where she lived. Once again, there is no record of the prosecution cross-examining the defense witness.

The defense next called former Alabama Public Safety Investigator B.J. Gatlin to testify. More than nine years after Buford Lolley's murder, Gatlin was employed as an investigator for Alabama's Third Judicial Circuit. He testified that he took a written statement from prosecution witness Fred Kellum in 1968, soon after Lolley was murdered. The investigator had no recollection of Kellum positively identifying a suspect leaving the gas station shortly after the murder. Gatlin's statement was consistent with Kellum's earlier testimony that he did not identify Hutto as a suspect until 1976, only after his wife wrote him a letter and urged him to contact ABI Investigator Weekley. There is no record of the prosecuting attorneys cross-examining Gatlin.

Inez Hutto took the witness stand on behalf of her son. She testified that David came home between 12:00 a.m. and 12:30 a.m. on January 14, 1968, went to bed, and never left the house until law enforcement arrived between 7:00 a.m. and 8:00 a.m. Like the three previous witnesses, there is no evidence the prosecution cross-examined Ms. Hutto.

David Hutto's sister, Frances Jerkins, was recalled as the next defense witness. Jerkins testified that her brother came home between 12:00 a.m. and 1:00 a.m. on the day of Lolley's murder. She also stated, "to the best of my knowledge," David did not leave home until after the police and state investigators arrived at the house between 8:30 a.m. and 9:00 a.m.

During brief cross-examination, the prosecution managed to point out time discrepancies between Frances and her mother concerning the actual arrival time of law enforcement officers at the Huttos' house on the morning of January 14th. It is unlikely the small difference in recollections about the actual time the police arrived at the Huttos' house diminished the believability of either witness as to David's whereabouts at the time of Lolley's murder.

Jerkins stepped down from the witness stand at 5:30 p.m. on Tuesday, March 29th, concluding testimony in the second day of the trial. After Judge Butts instructed the jurors not to discuss the case among themselves, they were escorted to the same motel. After adjournment, court was set to reconvene at 8:30 the following morning.

On the third day of the trial, the final defense witness was the defendant himself. On direct examination, Joe Pittman started out slow, inquiring about David Hutto's family and background. He then asked the witness whether he had ever been in "trouble with law." Hutto recalled being arrested for stealing a hog in 1968 and admitted to breaking into a school building in Zion Chapel, just north of Enterprise. Hutto also testified about escaping from a youth detention facility after he "had got the urge to go home and walked off."

When asked if he was familiar with the murdered gas station attendant, Hutto testified he knew Buford Lolley and "considered him to be a friend." He said that on the day Lolley was murdered, he returned to his mother's house between 12:00 a.m. and 1:00 a.m. The next thing he recalled was Chief Murdock awakening him in his bedroom, asking David where his clothes were and informing him "there had been a killing." If Hutto was to be believed, he had arrived home 2.5 to 3.5 hours before Lolley was killed.

Without hesitancy, Hutto testified he did not kill Buford Lolley and was unaware of the identity of the actual murderer. Hutto was adamant he "never" told anyone who killed Lolley. According to the defendant, if Patsy Hanks testified that she overheard him making statements that he was present at the Save-Way station on the morning of Lolley's murder and could identify the murderer, "she would be lying." Hutto testified he might have harbored a "suspicion" about who killed Lolley but "never said he knew who committed the murder." Hutto also made it clear he had cooperated with the police throughout the entirety of the murder investigation.

"Have you ever seen this before in anybody's possession?" Pittman asked the defendant, holding the murder weapon in front of him.

"No, I have not," Hutto replied.

On cross-examination, Assistant District Attorney Marsh asked the witness if all his prior crimes had been committed in 1968. When Hutto replied in the affirmative, Marsh first reminded the jury about Hutto's earlier testimony that he had been convicted of second-degree grand larceny and escape (from a youth detention center).

After Marsh confronted him about additional arrests, Hutto admitted he had been in "minor trouble" at earlier times in his life. Marsh's follow-up questions clarified Hutto's full criminal history and referred to his police record spanning from 1966 through 1976, which included convictions for public drunkenness, disturbing the peace, failure to appear, disorderly conduct, and assault and battery.

Hutto had no doubt significantly underplayed his prior criminal record. The exact nature of the assault and battery conviction, the only time Hutto was reported to have attacked someone, was not revealed by the press and cannot be recalled by the former assistant district attorney. Exactly how violent had he been? The jury had no difficulty understanding how Hutto's multiple arrests not only damaged his reputation and also made him well-known to local law enforcement officers prior to Lolley's murder.

As the cross-examination proceeded, Marsh asked Hutto if he remembered giving a statement to Investigator Gatlin that his girlfriend, Sue Ann Hawkins, had been with him at a dance in Samson the night before the murder. In his earlier testimony, Hutto had said that no girls had accompanied him to the dance. At this point, the defendant testified he could not clearly remember, indicating Hawkins may well have been with him "a portion of the night of the 13th."

When questioned about the alleged October 1968 alcohol and pot party, Hutto testified he had never been to Gladys Warren's house when Patsy Hanks was also present. Furthermore, there was "no way" Hanks could have been at the same party without his knowledge. In light of Hanks' earlier testimony that she overheard Hutto identify Lolley's killer, Marsh asked the defendant about the nature of his relationship with Billy Wayne Bradley. Hutto testified the two "had been" friends and sometimes hung out together and shot pool.

Marsh proceeded to ask the defendant if he ever said "I didn't kill him. Me and Belcher just got the money. Billy Wayne wouldn't have killed him if he hadn't woke up. Billy Wayne got mad because we threw the knife on the roof."

After Hutto emphatically denied making any of those statements, the assistant district attorney held up the murder weapon and asked the defendant if he had ever seen it. Hutto once again answered no. Marsh also asked him if he was aware Billy Wayne Bradley worked at a body shop in 1968, implying the weapon could have been crafted with an acetylene torch at the same location. Yet again, the witness replied in the negative.

After Marsh completed his cross-examination, the defense announced it was resting their case. The testimony of rebuttal witnesses would follow.

Talf and Bonnie Williams were the prosecution's first two rebuttal witnesses. Both testified they returned to Enterprise from the Dykes Club in Troy, 36 miles to the north, early on the morning of January 14, 1968. By that time of night, Talf had concluded his regular gig at the club, playing bass fiddle in a country music band.

The witnesses remembered arriving at the Save-Way gas station at approximately 1:45 a.m., accompanied by Ralph Adkinson, James H. Williams, and Gladys Warren. Talf and Bonnie recalled seeing David Hutto, Billy Wayne Bradley, and "another boy," all of whom remained at the station until as late as 2:00 a.m. or 2:05 a.m. Bonnie Williams testified Hutto was wearing a "brown, fleece-lined jacket" and Bradley was clad in a "sort of brown topcoat." Bonnie confirmed the coats looked much like those shown to her in pictures provided by the prosecution. It is uncertain how and when law enforcement obtained those photographs, and it is also possible the pictures Bonnie Williams referenced were really police sketches based on descriptions provided by Mary Lipford and possibly Fred Kellum.

The defense called J.P. Strickland as its lone rebuttal witness. Strickland testified he worked his regular evening shift at the Save-Way on January 13, 1968, and then stayed late to assist Buford Lolley. Strickland also stated he did not leave work until between 1:00 a.m. and 2:00 a.m. on the 14th. He was certain neither David Hutto nor Billy Wayne Bradley were present when the Williams' party arrived at the station. Strickland concluded Talf and Bonnie Williams were mistaken and must have stopped by the gas station earlier than they had previously testified.

During cross-examination, Marsh challenged Strickland about his actual departure time from the gas station on the morning of the murder. Strickland, however, refused to concede he left the Save-Way earlier than previously testified. In response, Marsh pointed out Strickland told investigators, a newspaper reporter, and a radio broadcaster that he left work around 1:30 a.m. or a bit later. Strickland, however, argued he never informed anyone in the media about leaving the gas station at or around 1:30 a.m. If Strickland had departed at an earlier time, it would have helped validate Talf and Bonnie Williams' testimonies about seeing Hutto and Bradley at the gas station at approximately 1:45 a.m.

WIRB radio station news reporter Bernie Cobb was called to the stand as the state's third and final prosecution rebuttal witness. Cobb testified that in a taped interview, J.P. Strickland had said he left the gas station at "1:30 a.m. or a few minutes after."

Following closing arguments by the prosecution and defense, Judge Butts charged the jury. As had been the case during opening statements, none of the details of lawyers' closing arguments were not published by the newspapers that covered the trial.

The jurors were instructed that a conviction of first-degree murder carried the penalty of a mandatory life sentence in prison. The jurors could also find Hutto guilty of second-degree murder, punishable by a mandatory penalty of not less than 10 years in prison. Lastly, the jury could find the defendant not guilty.

The jury began deliberating at 6:33 p.m. on Wednesday night, March 30, 1977. At 10:17 p.m., after nearly four hours of deliberations, jury foreman Ralph Pittman informed Judge Butts that they had not yet reached a verdict. At this point, the jury was sequestered for the night and ordered to return to the deliberation room at 8:00 the following morning.

On Thursday, the jurors deliberated throughout the day without arriving at a verdict. Around 5:00 p.m., the jury asked Judge Butts if they could again hear the testimonies of Fred Kellum and Mary Lipford. They also requested the judge repeat his charge concerning circumstantial evidence.

In took an hour for the court reporter, David Rhoden, to return with the requested testimonies. For the next two hours, he read aloud the earlier questions and answers to the jurors and a sizable number of spectators lingering in the courtroom. After repeating his charge on circumstantial evidence, Judge Butts ordered the jury to return to the deliberation room.

About a half hour later, the jurors returned to the courtroom. The exhausted foreman informed Judge Butts that the jury had not reached a verdict and "did not believe they could." Including time spent in sequestration, 28 hours had elapsed since the jurors received the case. After the jury was polled and unanimously agreed they were at an impasse, Judge Butts declared a mistrial in the murder case.

"I have determined that the jury is hopelessly deadlocked. I thank you for serving. You have been an attentive jury. You have been a good jury. You have been a conscientious jury," the judge announced, before dismissing them.

Containing his disappointment, Assistant District Attorney Dale Marsh informed reporters that David Hutto would be tried again during the next term of criminal court or at the first available opportunity. Marsh expressed hope that "other principals in the case" could also be brought to trial in the near future. The assistant district attorney asked anyone who might have additional information about the Lolley murder to contact ABI Investigator Weekley, District Attorney Stephens, or himself.

Reporters asked Judge Butts if the defendant's bond would be lowered prior to the next trial. The judge indicated he "could make no commitment until a formal request was made for such."

Many people who observed at least some of the trial were not surprised by the outcome. Jim Ellis, the long-time clerk of the court, recalled "the state's witnesses were weak and unreliable." A career law enforcement officer who attended a portion of the trial remembered "the investigation by the Enterprise Police Department was sloppy, and Chief Murdock was a terrible witness."

More than four decades after the first trial concluded, defense attorney Ken Hooks remembered it was not difficult to effectively cross-examine the witnesses testifying against Hutto. The defense attorney clearly recalled "there was no single event" that convinced jurors Hutto had committed murder.

"There was no meat to the prosecution's case," Hooks plainly stated.

Based on the lack of prosecutorial evidence, he believed "there never should have been a second trial." However, he was certain the district attorney's office was "hell bent" on prosecuting Hutto for murder.

Meanwhile, David Hutto returned to the Coffee County jail and continued to play the waiting game.

CHAPTER 9

The second trial

A T SOME POINT IN THE SIX weeks between his first and second trials, David Hutto was finally released on bail. To the best of Ken Hooks' recollections, a man of financial means who lived in Enterprise, perhaps a builder who had previously employed Hutto as a roofing subcontractor, stepped forward to guarantee the defendant's bail. Susan Hutto has the same memory about her husband's potential benefactor but was not positive about his name. If it was this particular individual, Hooks later stated that the man was wealthy and unpretentious and would have done what he thought was right, even if helping Hutto get out of jail was unpopular in certain local political and social circles.

Still an accused murderer, Hutto found it hard to find work. Circuit Judge Gary McAliley was perhaps the lone exception, hiring him to reroof his newly purchased home as well as an adjacent guest house.

On day one of Hutto's second murder trial, Monday, May 16, 1977, the early morning temperature was in the low 60s, but as the day progressed, the mercury climbed nearly 30 degrees. With very little breeze, it was unseasonably hot by afternoon. This stretch of summer-like weather persisted for the remainder of the week.

The trial venue was the same as the first: the second-floor courtroom in the white brick courthouse on Edwards Street. The major players were unchanged. Judge Terry Butts presided over the trial, while District Attorney Lewey L. Stephens, Jr. and Assistant District Attorney Dale Marsh led the prosecution. David Hutto's court-appointed lawyers, Joe Pittman and Ken Hooks, were once again responsible for defending their client.

On day one, 12 jurors—nine men and three women—were chosen from 31 candidates, a much smaller pool than was summoned for the first trial. It is possible Hutto's second trial, occurring only six weeks after the first one, was the only case on the docket, necessitating fewer jury summons. Dale Marsh, however, suggested another possibility for the small jury pool. Though not certain, he believes Hutto's criminal trial might have been added to a docket normally reserved for civil cases. If Marsh's recollection in accurate, the 31 prospective jurors would been drawn from the larger civil docket pool. While not certain, Terry Butts endorses Marsh's theory. Ken Hooks believes Marsh and Butts may be correct but doesn't discount the possibility that Hutto's second murder trial was the lone case during a special criminal court session, which would have also necessitated a much smaller jury pool.

During jury selection, Judge Butts asked: "Do any of you have a fixed opinion about conviction of a defendant based on circumstantial evidence?"

None of the prospective jurors answered yes. With a smaller group, it did not take long to select 12 jurors. As had been the case in the first trial, no alternates were qualified.

Dressed in blue jeans and black boots, Hutto sat at the defense table during jury selection. All the while, he smoked cigarettes and occasionally huddled for private conversations with his lawyers. In the interval between his two trials, Hutto had not changed his story one iota and was once again prepared to put his fate in the hands of his 12 fellow Coffee County residents.

Once the jury was selected, Judge Butts informed the panel they would likely begin deliberations in just two days. This trial was expected to be shorter because two key witnesses from the first one would not be returning to the courtroom. Instead, their earlier testimony from the previous trial would be read aloud to the jurors.

At the outset of the trial, Judge Butts instructed the prosecution and defense attorneys to avoid the heated exchanges that occasionally rose during the first trial. Instead, he ordered the lawyers to "address their remarks to the bench" and then await his ruling.

As was the case in the first trial, the content of the lawyers' opening statements was brief and not documented by reporters who were in the courtroom. Afterward, the state called Mary Lipford as its first witness.

Under direct examination by Assistant District Attorney Marsh, she testified she had been awakened by her then husband, Fred Kellum, at around 3:30 a.m. on January 14, 1968. Kellum asked if she heard someone calling for help. The witness remembered telling her husband the noise sounded more like "cats fighting."

Nonetheless, Lipford climbed out of bed and twice peered outside their bedroom window facing South Main Street, according to her testimony. At first glance, she did not notice anything unusual. However, when she returned to look out the window a second time, she saw "two boys" but could only identify them by their outerwear: a fleece-lined jacket and an all-weather topcoat. One of the two young men was standing outside the station, while the other was just inside the building and was bending over as if he was picking up something, Lipford said. Before long, both young men hurriedly walked across South Main Street in the direction of the Kellum's house.

Like the first trial, the defense would focus on the fact that Fred Kellum waited over eight years before informing law enforcement that he could positively identify David Hutto as one of the suspects leaving the scene of Lolley's murder. Consequently, during cross-examination, Joe Pittman asked Lipford if she had discussed reward money with her ex-husband.

"No, we did not," the witness answered.

Pittman elicited testimony from Lipford that her ex-husband *first* reported observing and identifying a suspect outside the kitchen window of their house only after ABI Investigator Steve Weekley had interviewed her. In the first trial, Lipford testified she wrote her ex-husband a letter after Weekley questioned her and urged Kellum to speak with the state investigator.

Lipford's cross-examination concluded with her declaring she had "worked with the police as best I could." By now, she appeared frustrated by the insinuation that she had been motivated to testify by the prospect of receiving a share of the reward money.

"I told them what I seen. I could not tell them who was at the station," she explained.

Lipford's testimony was the same as she delivered at the first trial. Of particular importance to the defense, she was unable to positively identify David Hutto or any other suspect on the morning of Buford Lolley's murder. In addition, Lipford informed jurors her ex-husband did not positively David Hutto as one of the suspects leaving the murder scene until he spoke with

Investigator Weekley, which resulted in an eight-year window between the commission of the crime and Kellum's most damaging testimony.

The next prosecution witness, former policeman Junior Farris, repeated his testimony from the first trial. He recalled driving by the Save-Way at 3:15 a.m. on the day of the murder, honking his horn, and observing Lolley wave back. There is no record of Farris being cross-examined by the defense.

Enterprise Police Department Lieutenant J.B. McDaniel took the stand next. He testified that his workload during the overnight shift on January 13–14 had been "pretty heavy," having already stopped 11 drunk drivers. McDaniel recalled stopping at the gas station at 3:37 a.m. to purchase a candy bar. After arriving at the Save-Way, he discovered a trail of blood leading from the front door to the back counter, where he found Lolley lying on the floor in a pool of blood. The police lieutenant vividly recalled blood was still "flowing" from Lolley's head wounds and the injury to his arm.

On cross-examination, after McDaniel testified that the person or persons who committed the savage murder would likely be covered with blood, the prosecution objected. After sustaining the objection, Judge Butts instructed the jury to disregard McDaniel's last statement.

After further questioning by the defense, McDaniel agreed he could not prove whether the trail of blood led to or from the front door. He also testified the "very uniform" trail of blood had not been covered by shoe prints. In addition, he remembered he first saw signs of blood on the concrete slab just outside the front door of the building. At the conclusion of Faris' and McDaniel's testimonies, neither the prosecution nor the defense appeared to have gained any clear advantage.

Former Alabama State Toxicologist Guy Purnell, who was living in Pennsylvania, could not be present for Hutto's second trial. Therefore, his testimony from the first trial was read aloud by Stephens and Marsh. Purnell, who performed Lolley's autopsy, discovered "at least seven wounds" on the decedent's body and determined the cause of death was brain damage due to "blows on the head" from "some type of heavy, blunt instrument."

Recitation of the toxicologist's earlier testimony showed that Purnell had been the one who discovered the cleaver-like murder weapon on the roof of the laundry across the street from the Save-Way station. Purnell's brief cross-examination from the first trial was also read aloud. The toxicologist had refused to offer an opinion about how much strength was needed to attack Lolley with the murder weapon. He also remembered receiving a two-dollar bill in the mail on January 31, 1968, from an anonymous source accompanied by a note requesting the currency be tested for blood. Purnell subsequently testified the two-dollar bill failed to yield any trace of blood.

Police Chief Howard Murdock was the last witness on the first day of the second trial. Murdock repeated most of his testimony from the first trial. Near the end, he recalled visiting Hutto's mother's house on the morning of the murder, intent upon examining the clothes David had been wearing when he returned home on night of January 13–14, 1968.

During cross-examination, when Joe Pittman showed Murdock a sketch of Mrs. Hutto's house, the police chief pointed out the absence of a fireplace in the drawing. When the defense attorney explained the fireplace had been closed up for years, Murdock refused to concede.

"That is one thing I remember about the house was that there was a fireplace right there when you went in," the chief declared in convoluted syntax.

The presence of a fireplace in the Mill Street house was difficult to prove. Defense witness Frances Jerkins, David Hutto's sister who lived in the home, said there was no fireplace. Another defense witness, Mrs. Ollie Drinkard, who had rented the same house previously, echoed Jerkins' testimony.

The defense team likely realized the longer Murdock testified, the more likely he was to offer confusing and contradictory statements. Pittman subsequently asked the chief if anything "stuck in the back of his mind" about visiting the Huttos' house the morning of Lolley's murder and would have been included in his written report.

"Yes, on the cold Sunday morning, that is was there had been washing done there," Murdock replied in a jumbled manner.

David's wife and daughter, who lived with Inez Hutto until her death, later remembered she routinely washed clothes quite early in the morning. As such, it would not have been an unusual occurrence on January 14, 1968.

After further questioning, Murdock testified he did not examine the washed clothes "because he did not have any authority, such as a search warrant, and didn't want to wear out his welcome." Just like during the first trial, Chief Murdock had contradicted himself. During direct examination, he testified that he went to the Huttos' house to examine David's clothes for blood stains. Under cross-examination, he testified he had neither the authority nor the willingness to intrude on the Huttos' hospitality long enough to actually examine the clothing. Adding to the confusion, Murdock testified in the first trial that he *did examine* the clothes Hutto had been wearing before he returned home and discovered *no blood stains*. It must have been extremely difficult for the jurors to draw any definitive conclusions about what the chief of police really observed at the Huttos' house on the morning of the murder.

At the request of the defense, Murdock read aloud the names of *20 suspects* tied to the Lolley murder case. *The Daily Ledger*, which provided the most comprehensive coverage of the trial and was the only newspaper to report that Murdock had recited a list of suspects, failed to furnish any of those names to its readers. In the first trial, the newspaper had also failed to document the names of the *eight to 10 suspects* read aloud by the police chief.

The defense soon returned to the issue of Murdock having proclaimed Hutto was innocent of murder. Pittman next asked the police chief if that same morning, he had informed David Hutto's mother that her son did not have to fear "being involved in the crime."

The chief tried to answer: "The way you are putting the words . . ."

Before Murdock could complete his sentence, the prosecution objected and was sustained by the judge. After Pittman pursued a similar line of questioning that failed to draw an objection from the prosecution, the police chief admitted, as he had done in the first trial, that he "might have made statements to that effect but that he did it to calm the woman, who was old and very worried about her son." Murdock proceeded to testify "any such statement" was not necessarily indicative of "the right conclusion." Murdock's testimony once again generated considerable confusion in the minds of the jurors.

Murdock's cross-examination wrapped up the first day of the trial. After directing the witnesses not to discuss the case among themselves, Judge Butts sent them under escort to their sequestration motel.

On Tuesday morning, prosecution witness Patsy Hanks testified for two hours. Repeating her testimony from the first trial, she recalled overhearing David Hutto talking about Buford Lolley's murder during a party hosted by Gladys Warren in October of 1968. According to Hanks, Hutto bragged that the police would never learn "how they went, where they went, or who killed Buford."

She also remembered Hutto saying: "Billy Wayne Bradley killed him, but me and Odell got the money."

In addition, Hanks offered testimony that she either did not share at the first trial or was not reported by the press. On the same morning Buford Lolley was murdered, Hanks recalled Enterprise Police Chief Howard Murdock visiting her home and providing her with a list of "17 boys in the neighborhood," asking her to "check them out and find out where they were that night and what they were wearing." Hanks further testified she visited the Huttos' home on the morning of the murder and noted David's mother had been washing clothes.

During cross-examination, Joe Pittman immediately attempted to weaken Hanks' credibility, suggesting her testimony was motivated by money. In a defiant tone, Hanks vowed she "would not take a penny of money." Not yet done exploring the possibility that a key prosecution witness had been paid to testify, Pittman asked Hanks if she had been renumerated by Chief Murdock or anyone in the police department, either in 1968 or closer to either of Hutto's murder trials.

Assistant District Attorney Marsh immediately objected to that line of questioning and was sustained by Judge Butts. Pittman soon followed with a similar question.

"The court sustained!" Marsh emphatically announced.

"Quit shouting at me!" Pittman responded.

"I have to shout at you to get your attention!" Marsh retorted.

Moving in a different direction that could possibly impeach the witness, Pittman asked Hanks about her brother, Billy Ray Myers, who was currently serving a 40-year jail term for felonies committed in Coffee County while also awaiting trial for additional charges in neighboring Dale County. Pittman questioned if the district attorney's office had offered to help her brother in exchange for testimony implicating David Hutto in the Lolley murder.

Hanks denied having received any direct offers of assistance from the prosecutors. She did, however, state her family had accumulated evidence suggesting Billy Ray had been framed and planned to present that information to the district attorney. As the unrelenting cross-examination proceeded, Hanks eventually admitted Chief Murdock once gave her $50, "but it was unrelated to the (Hutto) case."

In short order, the defense completed its cross-examination of the witness. If she could be believed, Hanks had again offered damning testimony against Hutto. Her veracity, at least in part, was an issue for the jurors to contemplate.

Since Sergeant Fred Kellum, who was now stationed as a military policeman in Germany, could not return in person for the second trial, Stephens and Marsh read aloud his direct and cross-examination testimony from the first trial. Kellum reported he was awakened at approximately 3:30 a.m. on January 14, 1968, by what he perceived as a cry for help. After looking out his bedroom and front windows, he saw nothing suspicious, according to his testimony. However, when Kellum went to the kitchen to pour himself a glass of water, he saw two "young men" pass by his window. He later identified one of them as David Hutto.

During cross-examination in the first trial, Joe Pittman confronted Kellum about why he did not share his identification of the suspect with the authorities immediately after the murder. Instead, the witness first informed ABI Investigator Weekley that he could identify Hutto as a suspect in the summer of 1976, *more than eight years* after the murder.

"If anyone could kill the old man, they wouldn't stop at hurting me or my family," Kellum answered.

"You were 27 years old then and afraid to cooperate with the police, but you let your wife go down and talk to them?" Pittman lambasted the witness during cross-examination in the first trial, which was read aloud to the jury and gallery during the second trial.

His character called into question, Kellum defended his decision. Since his wife had not seen the man's face, he "felt she was not in jeopardy."

During the second trial, when it came time came for Pittman and Hooks to present the defense's case, they relied heavily on David Hutto's testimony. His mother, Inez Hutto, however, did take the stand on Tuesday, testifying that David had remained in the house after midnight on the morning of Lolley's murder. She also remembered checking more than once to make sure he was asleep in his in bedroom. Mrs. Hutto also denied that Patsy Hanks visited her house on the morning of the murder, contradicting direct testimony from the prosecution's witness. Given that a mother was determined to protect her son, it is difficult to know how much weight the jury gave to her testimony.

Unlike during the first trial, Dale County Police Investigator John Nicholson and Patsy Hanks' siblings, Judy Grant and Jimmy Myers, were not subpoenaed by the defense team. By this point in the trial, individual and collective recollections are fuzzy, and newspaper coverage is particularly spotty. It is known that Gwendolyn Hutto, who was apparently another of David Kellum's ex-wives, was called as a defense witnesses. The nature of her testimony, however, is not known.

David Hutto was the last person called to the witness stand on Tuesday, where he remained for a bit over 75 minutes. Echoing his testimony from the first trial, Hutto claimed "he did not have anything to do with murder of Buford Lolley and did not know anyone who had anything to with the murder."

At least two witnesses confirmed that Billy Wayne Bradley was in the gallery, sitting in the windowsill of the crowded courtroom, during portions of one or both trials. It is not known if he was in the courtroom when Hutto testified. If he was present and closely monitored the defendant's every word, Bradley's physical presence could have intimidated Hutto. Much had changed since 1968. Hutto now had a wife and two young children in addition to his mother, all living under the same roof. It is not inconceivable that Hutto feared for the safety of his family if he implicated Bradley in the Lolley murder.

The defense and prosecution attorneys verbally sparred when Pittman asked the defendant if "anyone" might have talked to him while he was incarcerated at the Coffee County Jail about "implicating other persons in the murder." After a bench discussion between the lawyers and Judge Butts, Pittman was allowed to proceed with this line of questioning. Hutto testified that Police Chief Howard Murdock visited him in jail and asked about other people who might have been involved in the crime.

"Did Murdock tell you that he was satisfied that you did not commit the murder but that you knew who did?" Pittman asked.

"Yes," replied Hutto.

The prosecution immediately objected and was sustained by the judge, who instructed the jury to disregard the defendant's answer. When Pittman attempted to ask three similar questions, the prosecution objected and was sustained each time.

On cross-examination, Assistant District Attorney Marsh asked Hutto if he possessed enough strength to wield the steel weapon used to killed Lolley. The defendant replied the weapon was "much heavier" than the roofing hammers he was accustomed to using. Marsh also questioned the believability of Inez Hutto checking on her 19-year-old son who was sleeping in his bedroom after midnight on the day of the murder to make sure he was properly covered.

"She'll do it now if you don't watch her. You have to keep the door locked," Hutto replied, without hesitation.

The assistant district attorney also questioned the defendant about his mother's earlier testimony that the windows in her Mill Street house were nailed shut, even during the summer months. Marsh's implication was that Hutto could have snuck out of the house through his bedroom window and walked to the Save-Way station while his mother was watching a movie in the front room and would have been unaware of his absence.

"If you raised a window, she'd raise hell about it," Hutto responded.

Once the defense completed its direct witness examination, the state called its rebuttal witnesses. ABI Investigator Steve Weekley was among the first of the witnesses to testify. Weekley's direct testimony was neither documented by newspaper reporters nor remembered by courtroom observers.

On cross-examination, Pittman asked Weekley: "Has the word *reward* ever passed your lips in talking with any witnesses about this case?"

Weekley hesitated to answer, fearing he might mislead the jury. The defense attorney then asked for a simple yes or no answer.

"Yes," Weekley replied.

Talf and Bonnie Williams, who had testified at the first trial, were again called to the witness stand as rebuttal witnesses by the prosecution. Both recalled stopping at the Save-Way gas station at approximately 2:00 a.m. on January 14, 1968, to purchase gas, soft drinks, and cigarettes. Talf and Bonnie remembered seeing three "boys" at the station, identifying two of them as David Hutto and Billy Wayne Bradley. Neither witness knew the name of the third young man.

Bonnie testified Hutto was wearing a brown fleece-lined jacket and Bradley was clad in a topcoat. Her descriptions of both coats were consistent with those of prosecution witness Mary Lipford, who had observed two young men leaving the gas station shortly after the murder.

The descriptions of Hutto's coat, however, contradicted previous testimony from his mother and his sister, Frances Hutto Jerkins. Both women claimed David never owned a jacket like the one described by Bonnie Williams, and Mary Lipford. Inez Hutto went so far as to testify "none of her people" owned a brown fleece-lined coat and that she had never seen one like the two prosecution witnesses described. Ms. Jerkins testified her brother owned three jackets in 1968, all of them windbreakers. Consequently, the ownership of the brown fleece-lined jacket in question was never satisfactorily resolved.

During its rebuttal, the prosecution again raised the question about the fireplace. Patsy Hanks earlier testified that she overheard David Hutto saying he had burned his blood-splattered clothes in the fireplace at his mother's house on the morning of Lolley's murder. Franklin Harrison, who constructed Inez Hutto's rental house on Mill Street, testified as a rebuttal witness on behalf of the prosecution. The contractor told the jury that a fireplace was part of the house plan when the structure was built in 1946. According to Harrison, in the early years after the home was built, the fireplace was the only means of heating the house. He also testified the chimney was still standing when the house was torn down in the early 1970s. Much like the question about Hutto's jacket, the presence of a fireplace in the Huttos' Mill Street rental house was never verified. Today, there is no structure or even the remnants of a chimney on the vacant lot where the house once stood.

As a result of continuing rumors and allegations that law enforcement had paid Patsy Hanks to testify in both of David Hutto's murder trials, the prosecution called Enterprise Police Chief Howard Murdock back to the stand as a rebuttal witness. Because Joe Pittman was the city attorney and likely would not willingly embarrass the chief, the prosecution hoped Murdock would simply verify that the police department had not paid Hanks.

Much to the chagrin of the state, Murdock testified Hanks *had been paid $250* by the city of Enterprise for information about the murder of Buford Lolley. Under cross-examination by Joe Pittman, Murdock said he did not personally pay Hanks but was present in the mayor's office when she received the money. The chief, however, apparently never revealed the name of the person who allegedly paid Hanks. Rather than potentially strengthening the credibility of Patsy Hanks' testimony, Murdock only managed to muddy the water. In the opinion of a jurist who was present in the courtroom on that day, Murdock's confirmation that Hanks had been paid prior to testifying was a turning point in the trial and played a huge role in tilting the jurors toward an ultimate vote of acquittal.

Reflecting on the case more than 44 years after the trial, Dale Marsh was adamant that the district attorney's office never paid Hanks, which would have been a violation of the law. At the same time, he had no idea who might have given her money. According to Marsh, the most innocent yet unproven explanation for Hanks receiving money was for the purchase of some sort of "tape recording or bugging device" or other expenses she may have incurred. However, if she were being paid for services rendered to law enforcement, why was she paid in the mayor's office by someone other than a member of the police department?

The defense called James Williams, brother of Talf Williams, as their first rebuttal witness, aiming to impeach the earlier testimony of both his brother and sister-in-law. James testified that he, not Talf, had been driving the car when the group arrived at the Save-Way station early on the morning of the murder. While Bonnie Williams testified that Buford Lolley brought cigarettes to their car, James remembered walking inside the station to purchase the smokes. If Talf and Bonnie Williams could not recall who was driving the car and purchased the cigarettes, could they be relied on to verify the presence of David Hutto, Billy Wayne Bradley, and another unnamed youth at the gas station?

On cross-examination, Assistant District Attorney Marsh questioned James Williams' motives for testifying in the trial. Marsh implied there was "friction" between the witness and his wife because Williams had dated Patsy Hanks in 1968. The assistant district attorney specifically asked Williams if the reason he was testifying in this case was to "clear the air" with his wife.

"No, it is not," Williams replied.

When Marsh went through a series of rapid-fire questions about who was present at the station that early morning, Williams became confused. He contradicted himself more than once, first testifying Buford Lolley was at the station and later stating the attendant was not there. Williams also mistakenly referred to the Save-Way as the Bay Station. In the end, the state managed to call James Williams' testimony into question. Furthermore, he offered no eye-witness observations as to whether Hutto, Bradley, and another young man were at the gas station 90 minutes or so before Buford Lolley was murdered.

Night attendant J.P. Strickland was the next defense rebuttal witness. He recalled Talf and Bonnie Williams arriving at the Save-Way around 2:00 a.m. on January 14, 1968—15 minutes later than they had previously testified. He also recalled seeing David Hutto and "several other boys" at the gas station around 9:30 p.m. on January 13th but did not observe them at any point later in the evening or during the early-morning hours, further disputing the testimony of the Williams couple.

On cross-examination, the prosecution poked holes in Strickland's testimony, pointing out that the witness had previously recalled leaving the Save-Way at different times on the morning of Lolley's murder. On the witness stand, Strickland set his departure time between 1:30 and 2:00 a.m., but during interviews given to *The Daily Ledger* and radio reporter Bernie Cobb, the gas station attendant said he departed the Save-Way between 1:00 a.m. and 2:00 a.m. After being confronted with these inconsistencies, Strickland declared "you couldn't believe everything you read in the paper" and Cobb "must have been mistaken."

Now that the witness was on the defensive, the prosecution probed deeper, perhaps hoping to prove Strickland had embellished his story after Lolley was murdered. When questioned further, Strickland denied telling Chief Murdock and Investigator Weekley he had been carrying a gun out of fear that "he knew too much about the case and knew who killed Lolley." The witness also testified it was untrue he had shared his disapproval with Chief Murdock about how the police department was handling the murder case. Strickland also denied that he was unhappy when the chief failed to follow his recommendations about investigating potential suspects.

As the final prosecution rebuttal witness, Chief Murdock was recalled to the stand and questioned about Strickland's "reputation in the community for truth and veracity." Murdock testified Strickland's reputation was "bad," and he "would not believe him on his oath in a court of law." In the end, the prosecution managed to call into question the accuracy of Strickland's departure time from the Save-Way as well as his testimony about who was at the gas station in the early-morning hours prior to Lolley's murder. Strickland was also portrayed as an attention seeker, which further undermined his credibility.

After the testimony of rebuttal witnesses was completed, the prosecution was the first to deliver closing statements. District Attorney Lewey L. Stephens, Jr. informed the jury that the case against David Hutto, while circumstantial, was strong enough to convict him of murder.

"We don't know who struck that blow," Stephens explained, but challenged the jurors to look deep enough and "it will get down to the point that someone told you an untruth."

Stephens tried to shed doubt on Hutto's mother's testimony about her son's whereabouts at the time Buford Lolley was murdered. In the eyes of district attorney, Inez Hutto had provided a false alibi for her son.

"That the windows were nailed shut sent the ball over the fence, but that she went into a grown children's (sic) bedroom on the night of January 13–14 sent the ball slam out of the park," Stephens declared in a folksy manner.

In his closing statement, Assistant District Attorney Dale Marsh linked paper clips, one at a time, to demonstrate the accumulated evidence: the discovery of Buford Lolley's body, the discovery of the murder weapon on top of the nearby laundry, Mary Lipford seeing two boys at the Save-Way station, Fred Kellum identifying Hutto as he passed by his kitchen window, Patsy Hanks overhearing Hutto say he knew who killed Lolley, and Talf and Bonnie Williams recalling Hutto was at the gas station around 2:00 a.m. on January 14, 1968. Judge Butts clearly recalled Marsh's linking the paper clips to form a circle and demonstrating the chain of evidence. Years later, Butts still regarded Marsh's closing argument as imaginative.

During the state's closing arguments, David Hutto sat quietly at the defense counsels' table. He smoked cigarettes, made notes on a writing pad, and occasionally whispered to his attorneys. According to *The Daily Ledger*, Hutto "appeared a little nervous" during Assistant District Attorney Marsh's closing statement.

"The defendant constantly kicked his feet quietly against his chair or crossed his legs and swung one foot back and forth, motions not noticed during the previous trial time," the newspaper reported.

Joe Pittman delivered the initial closing statement for the defense. He immediately attacked a key prosecution witness, Patsy Hanks. Pittman declared that her testimony about never being paid any money for providing incriminating evidence against the defendant was "a bold-face lie." The defense attorney also reminded jurors that Hanks testified she overheard Hutto saying Billy Wayne Bradley was the actual murderer.

"If you believe that she quoted David Hutto correctly, you must believe that Billy Wayne Bradley killed Mr. Lolley and that he (Hutto) had nothing to do with the killing, except that he got the money," Pittman explained.

Pittman then enumerated the reasons for Hanks testifying in this case: "Number one, she is teed off with this system, the system we operate on, because her brother she perceives has been mistreated and still languishing in jail in Ozark to face two other charges. Number two, she's looking for the reward money she would not mention (but revealed) to her by Mr. Weekley, who said he had talked to the people he questioned about reward money."

The defense attorney informed the jurors that if Hutto was found guilty, it was tantamount to finding the other two young men, who were allegedly present at the scene of the crime, equally guilty. Consequently, if would be an injustice to pin responsibility for the murder on Hutto alone.

"The next logical step is to indict the other two," Pittman declared.

In his closing statement, Ken Hooks asserted the prosecution had "fallen short of its burden of proof in this case." Who could say, with any degree of certainty, that David Hutto had killed Buford Lolley?

"There is a complete void, a complete lack of any physical evidence whatsoever in this case," he proclaimed.

Hooks emphasized his point by quoting State Toxicologist Guy Purnell's report: "I know of no physical evidence which would link this suspect to the crime."

Specifically addressing the circumstantial evidence, Hooks argued: "In this case, the circumstances just don't add up. There are not enough circumstances to implicate this defendant."

Since the prosecution had the burden of proving the defendant guilty, Assistant District Attorney Marsh delivered the final statement to the jury. During his closing argument, he specifically focused on the defense's prior assertion about Hutto's alleged accomplices.

"Their time is coming when the evidence is put forth on them," Marsh proclaimed.

Hutto's fate now rested in the hands of 12 jurors. In his charge to the jury, Judge Butts explained there were three potential verdicts. The jurors could find Hutto guilty of first-degree murder, which carried a life sentence penalty. Secondly, the defendant could be convicted of second-degree murder, punishable by not less than 10 years in prison. As a third option, the jury could find Hutto not guilty.

The case went to the jury at 3:30 p.m. on Wednesday, May 18, 1977— nine years, four months, and four days after Buford Lolley was murdered. The jurors deliberated non-stop until 6:00 p.m. before asking Judge Butts if they could once again hear the testimony of Patsy Hanks.

While the court reporter prepared a tape recording of Hanks' testimony, the jury remained in the deliberation room. When the tape was ready, the jurors returned to courtroom and listened to the requested testimony. Why this witness' testimony was played on audiotape and all others were read aloud is not known.

Afterward, the jury adjourned to the deliberation room for only 15 minutes. Around 9:00 p.m., the jurors asked Judge Butts if they could resume their duties the following morning. The judge agreed and ordered them to return at 9:00 a.m. on Thursday.

For the third straight night, forewoman Jeanette Stinson and the 11 other jurors were escorted to the Enterpriser Motel by Coffee County Sheriff's Deputy Dan Simmons and Paula Alberson, an employee of the circuit clerk's office. The jurors would later send a letter to Coffee County Sheriff Neil Grantham praising the professionalism and politeness demonstrated by their sequestration caretakers.

While the jury deliberated and David Hutto awaited his fate, Patsy Hanks made her unhappiness known to the general public. The erratic prosecution witness telephoned both *The Daily Ledger* and WIRB radio, threatening them with lawsuits for reporting that she had received $250 from the city of Enterprise, paid by someone in the mayor's office, even after Chief Murdock had given sworn testimony about just such an occurrence.

At some point on Thursday afternoon, after deliberating throughout the day, the jurors asked to hear David Hutto's testimony once again. For just over an hour, court reporter David Rhoden read the testimony aloud. As he patiently waited, Assistant District Attorney Marsh fingered the interlocking paperclips he used during his closing argument.

At 5:30 p.m., after another round of deliberations, the jurors returned to the courtroom and informed Judge Butts that they were "hopelessly deadlocked." The judge, however, was not inclined toward declaring a second mistrial.

"At this point, I am not ready to let you stop." Butts instructed the jury.

After Butts sent them to eat supper, the jurors resumed deliberations at 7:20 p.m. At 8:15 p.m., the jury again asked to speak with judge. One of the older jurors, Greeley Bradley, informed the judge he "was not going to be able to make it" due to his "heart condition." Bradley contended he was being deprived of his regular diet and exercise regimen. Dale Marsh recalled Bradley was pale and perspiring, whether it was a result of his heart condition or a manifestation of anxiety. When the judge asked Bradley if he wished to see a doctor, the juror declined.

"I just want to go home," Bradley complained.

Judge Butts then asked for a show of hands as to how many jurors felt hopelessly deadlocked. Only three were raised in response to his inquiry.

"With only three saying you are hopelessly deadlocked, I can't see that you are," Butts responded.

Consequently, the judge ordered the jury to continue deliberating. In doing so, he evoked what is known as the Allen or "dynamite" charge. This charge is based on the premise that jury members, particularly those in the minority, must continue deliberations to avoid a mistrial. This charge had previously been upheld by the United States Supreme Court in 1896 (*Allen v. United States*).

At 9:20 p.m., after 15½ hours of deliberation and roughly 30 hours after receiving the case, the jury informed Judge Butts they had reached a verdict. At least two people later learned that the jury had previously voted 11 to one in favor of acquittal. Greeley Bradley, the juror with the heart condition, was the lone holdout for conviction. Bradley, however, changed his vote when the judge did not order a mistrial after considering his reported health issues.

After the jury forewoman passed the slip containing the verdict to Judge Butts, he read aloud: "We the jury find the defendant not guilty."

Even though the judge had warned against outbursts in his courtroom, David Hutto could not contain his joy. He slapped the tabletop, jumped out of his chair, and clapped his hands. While Susan Hutto shed tears of joy, other members of the Hutto family stood up and clapped their hands.

"I contended all along that I was innocent, but people stood by me, and I'm thankful for it," Hutto told *The Daily Ledger* reporter covering the trial.

When the journalist asked how he felt, Hutto exclaimed: "Wonderful. I don't know how to explain it. I couldn't have been prouder of anything."

"I am proud it's over. I want to thank everybody for standing by me. The press has been real good to me," he informed Bonnie Jepson, a reporter for *The Dothan Eagle*.

When asked about his prior felony convictions, Hutto chose to look forward: "I have been wrong before, but I paid for that, and I am trying to go straight."

Hutto also indicated he would continue to operate his roofing business in Enterprise: "Ain't nothing gonna run me off from my home."

Asked if his trial was fair, Hutto replied: "Yes, both times."

He further declared he had no bitterness against "anybody." In fact, the not-guilty verdict would prove to be a transforming moment in Hutto's life.

"I'm glad it's over and out of my life," he proclaimed to those within earshot.

Hutto also thanked his court-appointed lawyers, Joe Pittman and Ken Hooks: "I couldn't have searched the United States over and got two better ones. They're marvelous; they done a good job."

Save-Way gas station owner Leon Devane's son, Vance, remembered being in the courtroom when the verdict was announced. He admittedly felt "some disappointment because I wanted justice done for Buford."

Leon Devane, who knew both David Hutto and Billy Wayne Bradley, was not "shocked or mad" about the verdict. According to Vance, his father never offered a definitive opinion about who murdered Lolley but was "convinced Hutto did not do it."

"He thought the *other guy* did it," Vance remembered.

On the losing side of the case, Assistant District Attorney Dale Marsh was diplomatic: "The state is satisfied that this matter has been resolved by a dedicated, hard-working jury. It is obvious from the requested testimony, which was read back, and many hours of deliberation, that the verdict was reached."

More than 44 years after Hutto's acquittal, Marsh recalled that the district attorney's office suspected Billy Wayne Bradley was "guilty but could not produce enough evidence to obtain a grand jury indictment." Consequently, there were no further indictments, arrests, or trials related to Buford Lolley's murder. After taking into consideration testimony by Police

Chief Howard Murdock that Patsy Hanks had been paid by an unknown person in the mayor's office, Marsh still does not believe there was any orchestrated cover-up or malfeasance on the part of law enforcement.

"We just wanted justice done," Marsh reflected.

District Attorney Lewey L. Stephens, Jr., however, was incensed by the verdict. As he was driving away from the courthouse, accompanied by Coffee County Sheriff Neil Grantham, Stephens accidently sat on the microphone attached to his automobile's police band radio, inadvertently keying the transmitter. For miles, law enforcement agents overheard the district attorney, as one local resident described it, "raising hell at Chief Murdock," whom he held responsible for the prosecution losing the case. The district attorney's rant proves that even murder trials can have moments of levity. One can only imagine what was running through the minds of law enforcement agents listening to Stephens' biting remarks over the airways.

A local lawyer, who had watched the proceedings from the gallery, had suspected Hutto would be acquitted. In his mind, the "credibility of the prosecution witnesses were called into question." Inarguably, three of the four key witnesses testifying for the state had credibility issues. Chief Howard Murdock was indecisive and contradictory. Patsy Hanks, in addition to having her veracity called into question, was tainted by allegations that she was paid before testifying. Even Fred Kellum's explanation about waiting more than eight years before identifying Hutto as one of the suspects could be called into question simply based on the delay and the possibility of receiving reward money.

The end result was freedom for David Hutto, and a murder case that will likely remain forever cold.

CHAPTER 10

I am trying to go straight.

In July of 1978, 14 months after he was acquitted of murdering Buford Lolley, David Hutto's heart must have skipped a beat or two when he received a letter from the Office of the Clerk of the 12th Judicial Circuit Court. What could they possibly want now?

The notice was a judgment for $1,526—the amount the government paid Joe Pittman and Ken Hooks for representing him during his two trials. It was routine for the state of Alabama to seek payment from indigent persons who had been represented by court-appointed attorneys. Like most other recipients of such judgments, Hutto lacked the funds to repay the legal fees, ignored the order, and apparently heard nothing more from the circuit clerk's office.

For a decade or more, while David continued roofing houses, money remained tight in the Hutto household. David, Susan, and their two children, Kim and Chris, continued to live with Inez Hutto in a series of rental homes. The family was frequently on the move. Whenever Inez decided a landlord had raised the rent too much, she relocated the Hutto clan to another residence. While growing up, Kim remembered living in two different houses on the same street in Enterprise.

For years, Inez was the glue holding the Hutto family together. Her son, daughter-in-law, and two grandchildren continued to live with her until Inez's death from complications of diabetes and possibly a stroke on April 5,

1990. Coincidentally, Inez died on the same day of the week and month that she had married her husband, who predeceased her 29 years earlier.

The Hutto family's closeness was based not only on love but also practical considerations. Because their various rental houses were not spacious enough for Kim to have her own bedroom, she slept with her grandmother until she was 14 years old.

"I still miss her terribly," Kim reminisced, 21 years after Inez Hutto passed away.

After his mother's death, Hutto arranged to have his father's body moved from a cemetery in Henry County, near the town of Abbeville, where David was born. Thomas Hutto, who died in 1961, was reinterred next to his wife at Meadowlawn Cemetery on the southern outskirts of Enterprise.

According to family members, David never dwelled on the fact that he had twice been tried for murder. If he ever felt sorry for himself, he refused to let it show. According to Susan, her husband simply wanted to "get on with life." Forever convinced he had been set up to take the fall for Buford Lolley's murder, David rarely displayed any bitterness. Susan, however, has never forgiven Steve Weekley, believing the ABI investigator arrested her husband for a crime he knew David didn't commit.

Hutto continued to drink heavily for a time after the 1977 trials, but there is no documentation of subsequent arrests. His post-trial vow, "I am trying to go straight," proved to be more than just empty words. According to his daughter, David "grew up" after his mother died. For the first time in his life, David, who was 43 years old, became the acknowledged head of the household. Eventually, he stopped drinking, a habit that had no doubt contributed to many of his past misjudgments and indiscretions.

None of David's family remembered other members of the community ostracizing him about having once been accused of murder. At the same time, Hutto never openly expressed discomfort about his youthful indiscretions. He chose to judge others based on their current behaviors, and he expected reciprocity. Kim specifically remembered her father "didn't dwell" on the past and was quite "satisfied that he was found innocent" in court.

"One day, the good Lord will settle this," David had said to his daughter.

In addition to being a hard worker, Hutto was a loving husband and father. If the weather was not oppressively hot, in order to spend more time with his young children, David sometimes had Kim and Chris accompany him to his work sites. Hutto continued roofing houses until his back could no longer handle the strain, sometime in the late 1980s or early 1990s. He was eventually diagnosed with ankylosing spondylitis, a rare inflammatory arthritis that usually starts in the back before spreading to the neck. As the disease progresses, it damages the spine, causes chronic pain, and often forces its victims to assume stooped postures. After his career as a roofer ended, David worked for a time at James Hines' gas station and Forehand's Auto Parts.

In 2000, David purchased Annie's Café on North Main Street. A combination restaurant and pool hall, the business derived its name from its original owner. David started out working at Annie's as the part-time night manager while still working his regular day jobs before he accumulated enough funds to buy the eatery. David and Susan later purchased the Koffee Kettle, a diner akin to Waffle House, located on Fort Rucker Boulevard. In retrospect, Kim believes owning and operating restaurants was her father's favorite occupation.

Susan Hutto helped out at both restaurants, once working 24 straight hours at the Koffee Kettle after several employees walked out over a long-forgotten dispute. In addition, she was employed by Walmart and later by Grocery Advantage.

When asked by her daughter what she liked to do for fun, Susan replied: "I go to work, and I go to church."

Susan's credo is summed up by the words written on a small sign kept close at hand wherever she has been employed: "Work is my happy place."

Although David never finished high school, he encouraged his children to pursue their education and supported their extracurricular activities. Kim, who was a member of the high school marching band, recalled her father never missed the group's half-time performance, even if he skipped the first and second halves of the football game.

Kim attended a local community college and earned her degree as a certified medical assistant. Chris, a talented artist who is particularly adept at drawing portraits, briefly attended the Art Institute of Atlanta but never completed his degree. His career has included stints at Utility Trailers, Sessions peanut mill, Alfab (a company manufacturing aluminum and steel dump truck bodies, trailers, and oilfield equipment), as well as operating a pawn shop. Kim's daughter, Taryn, also graduated from community college and works as an ultrasound technologist.

The Huttos operated Annie's Cafe until 2008, when they sold the eatery. Today, under different ownership and minus the pool tables, the restaurant continues to be a popular Main Street dining venue. David eventually sold the Koffee Kettle as well. After retiring from the food service industry, he spent his later years working part-time at his son's pawn shop in Enterprise. At some point, David was forced to apply for Social Security disability because of the progressive ankylosing spondylitis.

David spent as much time as possible with his three grandchildren, Tanna, Taryn, and Connor. Taryn established a particularly close bond with her grandfather, especially after Kim returned to work following her daughter's birth. In the years before he sold the eateries, David looked after Taryn daily, carrying her in tow as he traveled back and forth between Annie's and the Koffee Kettle. Once Taryn started school, David dropped his granddaughter off in the mornings and picked her up in the afternoons. According to Kim, David and Taryn forever remained "best buddies."

Devoted to family first and foremost, Hutto tended to have more acquaintances than close friends. He did maintain a lifetime friendship with Runt Qualls (his co-conspirator in the 1960s hog theft caper) and Runt's twin brother, Red. He also enjoyed long-term relationships with brothers Bobby Gene and Robert Thomas as well as Ray Milligan. According to Kim, her father met regularly with members of this close-knit group to drink coffee and "shoot the bull."

Like his father before him, David had been an excellent roofer. In fact, his prized hammer boasted Thomas Hutto's thumb print imbedded in the wooden handle. But when it came to performing basic household repairs, Hutto displayed little interest or inclination. When finances allowed, he preferred to pay a handyman to undertake those tasks.

David's hobbies were mostly simple, with minimal variation. He read the newspaper every day, but his daughter rarely recalled her father opening a book, except for the Bible. His television viewing menu consisted mainly of westerns, University of Alabama football games, police dramas, *Pawn Stars*, and Dothan's WTVY evening news.

His overriding passion, however, was trading cars. According to his son-in-law, Terry Mitchell, David loved to "buy, trade, and swap" automobiles.

More than once, he left home in the morning driving one car and returned later in the day behind the wheel of another. Sometimes, he would sell or trade a recently purchased vehicle before original title transfer paperwork had been completed. When Kim was 16 years old, her father bought her a used Ford Pinto, which he spray-painted blue. For the next three years, until she could afford to purchase her own vehicle, Kim drove 19 different automobiles. Hutto was the ultimate "car flipper." With a talent for negotiating prices and calculating sales taxes in his head, David was adept at turning a profit while trading cars, which was certainly helpful when family finances were tight.

On at least one occasion, Hutto's propensity for buying, selling, and trading extended beyond automobiles. Terry recalled David purchasing a lawn mower and then selling it before his son-in-law had the opportunity to cut the grass.

With his thin physique, David never had to exercise and saw little need to break into an unnecessary sweat. Even as a middle-aged adult, David stood only five-feet, seven-inches-tall and weighed 120 to 130 pounds. He purchased his attire in the young men's section of clothing stores, preferring to wear blue jeans but switching to khakis to attend church services. In the summertime, he donned cut-off jean shorts. All of David's shirts, regardless of the style, had a chest pocket to accommodate a pack of cigarettes. Never a clothes horse, Hutto wore tennis shoes or comfortable slip-ons, mostly the latter as he grew older and progressive spinal stiffness from the ankylosing spondylitis made it difficult for him to bend over and tie his laces.

Kim remembers seeing her father wearing a necktie only twice. The first occasion was at a relative's wedding. At his daughter's wedding, if not entirely of his own choosing, David donned a tuxedo and bow tie.

David's taste in food was simple, but he was always a picky eater. He rarely consumed meat, even to the point of consuming only thin-crust pizzas with minimal or no meat toppings. He was a fan of spaghetti but avoided meatballs. He never drank regular milk, to the point of eating dry breakfast cereal. Instead, he consumed large amounts of buttermilk or combined it with cooked canned biscuits to create a mushy concoction, which he devoured. He always preferred to make his own French fries, hand-cutting baking potatoes into the desired length and thickness. Rather than ketchup, David always dipped his fries in Heinz 57 steak sauce. After he stopped drinking alcohol, his beverages of choice, in addition to buttermilk, were Coca-Cola, coffee, and sweet tea.

Like so many others, David was not without his share of peculiarities, and according to his daughter, he "always liked things done a certain way." He insisted on being the first one in the family to read the newspaper, and when the pages were turned, David maintained a precise fold and perfect crease. When opening a loaf of bread, he would compulsively reach well into the stack of slices before selecting his own, lest another person had previously touched the topmost pieces.

Regarding himself as a "common man," David had no use for pretense. He purposefully avoided so-called "snooty people." At the same time, he took special care to never make anyone feel self-conscious about their appearance or unusual mannerisms, perhaps the result of having lived with strabismus for much of his own life. Loath to "hurt someone's feelings," David had particular sympathy for individuals who were handicapped or otherwise physically disabled.

Unable to afford expensive veterinarian bills, which limited his ability to be an indulgent pet owner, Hutto was nonetheless fond of dogs, particularly Boston terriers. Moreover, he would not abide the mistreatment of animals.

From a political perspective, David was decidedly a conservative Republican. Later in life, he took the necessary steps to have his felony record expunged so he could legally purchase a firearm and regain his voting privileges. According to his granddaughter Taryn, Hutto planned to vote for Donald Trump in November of 2016 but did not live long enough to cast what likely would have been his first and only ballot in a presidential election.

With the passage of time, Hutto's ankylosing spondylitis worsened, increasing his pain and reducing his mobility. He also developed repetitive deep venous thromboses (blood clots in the lower legs that can cause death if they circulate to the heart, lungs, or brain). However, David's most serious health condition, and the one that cut his life short, was largely self-induced.

Although he gave up alcohol, Hutto never overcame his addiction to nicotine. For most of his adult life, he smoked at least two packs of cigarettes per day. When tobacco prices increased, he simply switched to the cheapest brands of cigarettes available. While Susan Hutto gave up smoking years earlier, her husband lacked the desire or willpower to follow in his wife's footsteps.

Years of smoking, perhaps coupled with a genetic predisposition to lung disease, led to severe chronic obstructive pulmonary disease. As his lung function diminished, David became dependent on supplemental oxygen and was forced to restrict his physical activities. On February 11, 2006, when his lungs failed him, David Hutto died at the age of 67.

His passing marked the end of a colorful and controversial life, a life in which he was acquitted of committing the most heinous of crimes and yet made the most out of his days without feeling rancor or seeking martyrdom.

CHAPTER 11

Reexamining a very cold case

W HO KILLED BUFORD LOLLEY IN THE early-morning hours of January 14, 1968? The answer will most likely never be known for certain. More than a half-century has passed since the crime was committed, and the likelihood of a previously unheard eyewitness emerging or the actual killer confessing, while not impossible, is extremely remote. Furthermore, there is a distinct possibility that Lolley's murderer is now deceased.

A plausible but unproveable theory is that Buford Lolley might not have been the killer's intended target. Shortly after the homicide, an ABI investigator told Save-Way owner Leon Devane, who was known to carry $3,000 to $4,000 in cash in his wallet, that he may have been the person the robbers hoped to encounter on that bitterly cold Sunday morning. Perhaps the perpetrators mistakenly struck an hour too early, as Devane was known to arrive at his gas station at 4:30 a.m. each day. Miscalculated timing, however, is only a theory. The reality is that Lolley was the victim of a murderer's wrath.

More than a half-century later, who should be considered the prime suspects? While David Hutto was indicted, arrested, and tried for the murder nine years after Lolley was killed, two juries failed to convict him of the crime. In the spring of 1977, over the course of roughly two months, the first jury panel could not agree on a verdict, resulting in a mistrial. The second trial ended in an outright acquittal. The fact Hutto was never found guilty of murder is noteworthy since jurors at that point in time tended to favor the prosecution. Yet, neither jury concluded there was enough evidence to convict Hutto. Since his acquittal, there apparently have been no serious efforts to search for Lolley's murderer, resulting in what is now a very cold case.

In five-plus months, beginning with his arrest and ending in his ultimate acquittal, David Hutto never wavered from the basics of his story: he did not kill Buford Lolley and could not identify the killer. More than five decades later, the available evidence supports his claims, at least in part.

While Hutto was no saint in his late teens and early 20s, all but one of his arrests involved offenses where there were no acts of violence directed toward another person, including burglary, theft, public drunkenness, and repeated episodes of driving under the influence of alcohol. During his murder trials, the state brought forth evidence that Hutto had once been convicted of assault and battery, but no details were revealed. Dale Marsh, who informed the jury about Hutto's prior criminal history, has no recollection of the nature of the defendant's assault and battery charges.

There is no evidence to suggest Hutto behaved in a vicious or cruel manner, and if his prior assault and battery arrest had involved significant injury to others, the local press never reported it. Multiple people who were Hutto's youthful contemporaries describe him as a person who would not shy away from fights if provoked but never deliberately sought out violent confrontations.

Hutto's wife and daughter, while not necessarily the most unbiased of sources, agree with this assessment of his character. David's daughter, Kim, freely admitted her father had his "share of bar fights" but has always maintained he "never killed anyone." His wife, Susan, who knew Hutto better than anyone else, described him as "calm and easy going," with a long fuse. According to Susan, David would only try to "whip your ass" if someone besmirched the reputation of his loved ones.

Given his short stature and rail-thin physique, Hutto was hardly the protype for a heavyweight boxer, professional wrestler, or barroom bouncer. Judge Gary McAliley, who trusted Hutto enough to hire him as a roofer in the interval between the first and second murder trials, when the defendant's reputation and character had been seriously called into question, emphatically stated David "wouldn't take crap from anyone but wouldn't look for a fight."

McAliley went a step farther, characterizing Hutto as a "smart, little-bitty man" and one who "never raised his voice."

Ray Milligan, a Maryland native who was just over a year younger than Hutto, is a military veteran who was stationed in Vietnam in 1968, the same year Buford Lolley was killed. Milligan and Hutto later developed a friendship lasting for more than 25 years, until Hutto's death. The two men spent many hours drinking coffee together and conversing about past and present events.

Milligan offered a frank assessment of Hutto's personality: "He was always honorable and a good friend to me. He was never dark, but he wasn't overly optimistic either."

"David was a little outspoken," Milligan recalled but at the same time was certain far more people liked Hutto than not.

Milligan recalled Hutto rarely spoke about his involvement in the Buford Lolley murder case. David did bring up the subject at least once, telling his friend he "spent four months in the Elba jail for something I didn't do." In no uncertain terms, Hutto professed his innocence, believing "someone set me up."

"I would never do anything like that," Hutto explained to his friend.

Milligan believed Hutto was being truthful: "I never saw him lose his temper bad enough to punch someone. The most I saw him do was get irritable. Even if David told me he killed someone, I would still have a hard time believing it. He was not capable of doing something like that."

During two murder trials, the prosecuting attorneys' determined efforts to convict Hutto were hampered by more than one ineffectual witness. Patsy Hanks was described by one Enterprise lawyer as "rough, loud-mouthed, haughty, and cocky." While Hanks' testimony incriminated both Hutto and Billy Wayne Bradley, her own brother openly testified he wouldn't believe a thing she said. In addition to her less-than-stellar reputation in the community, Hanks' testimony was further tainted by Police Chief Howard Murdock's testimony that she was paid prior to the murder trials by an unknown party, in of all places the office of the mayor of Enterprise. Hanks also made dramatic but unverifiable claims that she was threatened with physical harm if she testified against Hutto.

Chief Murdock was an ineffectual and contradictory witness. Most often, he appeared woefully unprepared when taking the witness stand. His conflicting answers to the same or similar questions likely left jurors far more confused than enlightened.

Fred Kellum's claim of seeing David Hutto leaving the scene of the murder in the early-morning hours of January 14, 1968, was clouded by the fact that he didn't share the information with ABI Investigator Steve Weekley until more than *eight years* after the crime. If Kellum's identification of Hutto was accurate, it occurred late in the game and after the prospect of reward money was placed on the table.

Mary Lipford was the most reliable of the key prosecution witnesses, but the most incriminating portion of her testimony was limited to seeing "two boys" departing the Save-Way Station near the time of the murder. Even then, Lipford could only identify the suspects by their outerwear.

Rebuttal witnesses, subpoenaed by both the prosecution and the defense, offered contradictory testimonies. As a result, jurors heard conflicting accounts about the presence of three young men at the Save-Way gas station shortly before the murder, two of whom were identified as David Hutto and Billy Wayne Bradley.

Based on Hutto's repetitive arrests, it is not unreasonable to conclude that as someone who was well-known to local law enforcement as a rowdy drunk who lived near the site of a murder, he was a convenient target for indictment, arrest, and prosecution. Ambitious and driven to solve a nearly nine-year-old cold case, ABI Investigator Steve Weekley may have concluded Hutto was at the scene of the crime but was not the killer. If enough pressure was applied to Hutto during his pre-trial incarceration and when he was on the witness stand, Weekley and the prosecuting attorneys may have reasoned Hutto would eventually break down and finger the true murderer.

However, if Hutto feared Lolley's killer might retaliate by targeting his loved ones, he had strong motivation not to change his story. At the same time, he never asked his attorneys about any possibility of a plea deal. Instead, he twice rolled the dice, hoping juries would find him innocent of committing murder.

Described by a former Enterprise Police Department officer as a "follower who did not want confrontation or violence," Hutto repeatedly told his lawyers he was innocent and had no knowledge about who murdered Lolley. While under oath, he never wavered. After subpoenaing several witnesses whose credibility and reliability were open to doubt, the prosecution was unable to convince two juries, after lengthy deliberations, that David Hutto was guilty of committing murder.

After he was acquitted, Hutto vowed to "live straight," a promise supported by the absence of subsequent criminal acts, a solid work history, and his unwavering devotion to his family. Eventually, Hutto stopped drinking alcohol, a disinhibiting lubricant that likely fueled his prior commission of criminal acts. In time, he successfully petitioned for his felony record to be expunged, allowing him to purchase a firearm and register to vote.

For the remainder of his life, Hutto largely preferred to leave the past in his rear-view mirror and withstood any temptation to mount a soapbox and publicly declare his innocence or proclaim he was wronged by the legal system. At some point, he privately contacted Karen Hudson Miller, whose aunt was Buford Lolley's sister-in-law. According to Miller, who is a volunteer at the Pea River Historical Society and a prominent contributor to the Facebook page "Celebrate Enterprise," Hutto learned of her family's close relationship with Buford Lolley via the same social media platform. Hutto particularly wanted her to know he "didn't kill Buford." Prior to hearing directly from Hutto, Miller recalls numerous people describing David as a "likeable guy and not capable of murder."

While never achieving financial prosperity, Hutto worked hard and took care of his family. Numerous people who had personal or business relationships with Hutto had nothing negative to say about his character or reputation. More specifically, none of them believe Hutto was the type of person capable of committing murder. While opinions are not an exact science and cannot be relied on to establish guilt or innocence, their cumulative value cannot be entirely discounted.

John McCrummen, who was born and raised in Enterprise, works in financial services and is also an ordained minister. Having long dealt with individuals of questionable veracity, McCrummen, one of the ministers who officiated David Hutto's funeral, considers himself a good judge of character. Near the end of Hutto's life, McCrummen asked David, point blank, if he killed Buford Lolley. When Hutto answered no, the preacher believed him.

If Hutto was not the murderer, was he one of the robbers who was at the scene of the crime? While he never admitted to law enforcement officers, prosecutors, his own defense attorneys, or family members that he was present at the Save-Way gas station at or around 3:30 a.m. on January 14,

1968, Hutto later privately told at least one person he *knew* the identity of the killer. This admission came after his acquittal, when Hutto had nothing to gain from a legal perspective.

Given that Hutto was not braggadocios by nature, how could he be certain about the killer's identity, unless he *actually witnessed* Lolley's murder? Was he one of the two suspects seen leaving the gas station in the wake of the murder, crossing South Main Street, briefly pausing at the Enterprise Laundry, and tossing the murder weapon on the roof? If so, Hutto could have continued east on Erin Street, turned right on Mill Street, and arrived at his mother's house, only 0.2 miles from where Buford Lolley was bludgeoned to death.

Fred Kellum's more than eight-year delay before informing authorities about what he saw on the morning of Lolley's killing is no doubt troublesome. Nonetheless, Kellum, who lived at the corner of South Main and Erin Streets, testified under oath that he could positively identify Hutto as one of the suspects leaving the gas station after hearing Buford Lolley's dying plea. And someone, even if it was not Hutto, was responsible for discarding the murder weapon on top of the laundry across the street from Kellum's residence.

Well-known to local law enforcement officers prior to Lolley's murder, Hutto was considered a suspect long before Fred Kellum identified him. Despite an inefficient search of the premises and only partial questioning of the people who were present, Enterprise Police Chief Howard Murdock was suspicious enough about David's potential involvement in the crime to visit Hutto's mother's house just a few hours after Lolley's murder.

If any portion of Patsy Hanks testimony can be believed, Hutto placed himself at the scene of the crime. While Hanks testimony must be taken with a grain of salt, but she did report overhearing Hutto admit the following: Billy Wayne Bradley killed Buford Lolley after he awoke from his nap, Bradley was angry that the murder weapon was tossed on top of the Enterprise Laundry (which suggests he was not the one who actually discarded it there), and Hutto and Odell Belcher (presumably the third youth) made away with at least part of the money stolen from the gas station. Efforts to locate Odell Belcher or interview anyone familiar with him proved unsuccessful.

After Hutto was acquitted of murder, a respected attorney discussed the case with the lawman who arrested him: "Steve Weekley told me that Hutto didn't do it, but that David damn well knew who killed Lolley. They charged David Hutto, hoping he would squeal on the actual murderer."

That same lawyer, who came to know Hutto quite well, directly asked him if he had killed Lolley. Without hesitation, Hutto responded he did not commit the murder, but he *knew* who did it. Again, how could Hutto have been certain of that fact unless he was at the scene of the crime?

While no one but the perpetrators or a yet-unidentified eyewitness can ever verify who did what on the night of the robbery and murder at the Save-Way gas station, sufficient evidence points toward Hutto being present at the scene of the crime. However, it appears unlikely Hutto committed the murder.

What about Billy Wayne Bradley? None of the individuals who vouched for David Hutto's character had anything positive to say about Bradley. Several youths, who were approximately the same age as Bradley, remember being instructed by their parents and peers to stay away from him. A sampling of descriptions about Bradley's character by those who knew him is anything but flattering: "He was a terrible, terrible person." "He wasn't worth a shit." "He was a glutton for attention."

At five-feet, nine-inches-tall and weighing roughly 200 pounds, Bradley would have been a more formidable killer than Hutto, particularly when using a cumbersome steel weapon to beat a man to death. By all accounts, Bradley's capacity for committing aggressive acts was well-established long before Lolley's murder. In addition, Bradley's disposition was known to grow nastier when he was intoxicated, which apparently was a frequent occurrence. Overindulgence in alcohol has long been known to disinhibit and individual's judgment, words, and actions.

According to a retired law enforcement agent who actively worked the case, a cashed check bearing Billy Wayne Bradley's signature was found in the Save-Way cash register on morning of Lolley's murder. Unfortunately, there was no time stamp on the check, which was drawn from Enterprise's Citizens Bank. Nonetheless, the presence of the check established that Bradley was inside the gas station shortly before the murder occurred. If Save-Way's business-savvy owner Leon Devane made a Saturday-morning bank deposit, Bradley's check is a strong indicator that he was present at the station less than 24 hours before Lolley's murder.

It has been reported by several sources that Bradley left town soon after Lolley's murder. Precisely where he went and how long he stayed away from Enterprise are not known. In contrast, David Hutto remained in the same place for the rest of his life. Bradley died in the panhandle of Florida; Hutto passed away in the Enterprise area.

It has been established by more than one source that Bradley's father owned a machine shop equipped with an acetylene torch, located within easy walking distance from the Save-Way station. Was the murder weapon crafted there? If Bradley was one of the three youths seen at the gas station in the early-morning hours of January 14, 1968, is it possible he did not join the other two in crossing South Main Street, passing by the Enterprise Laundry, and continuing toward Mill Street? Instead, did Bradley park his automobile at his father's business and drive 1.5 miles to his residence at 203 West Huey Street immediately after the murder?

There is no doubt Bradley was capable of violence. Judge Gary McAliley remembered granting Bradley's wife a divorce on the grounds of physical abuse. According to McAliley, Bradley "beat up" his wife and clearly recalled "seeing marks" on her, substantiating her claims of physical abuse.

"I would not doubt Billy Wayne Bradley killed Buford Lolley," McAliley explained, without hesitation.

A former Enterprise policeman who was familiar with both Billy Wayne Bradley and David Hutto described the latter as "sly as a snake, but not stupid or aggressive." The same retired lawman has long-believed Bradley murdered Lolley.

"He was a mean son of a bitch. He had that kind of personality: evil," the ex-policeman proclaimed, without reservation.

Billie Patrick spent a portion of her childhood living next door to Bradley and his parents. She clearly recalled just how "mean" Billy Wayne was as a seven- and eight-year-old child.

"Most everyone I have talked to over the years thinks he was the one who killed Mr. Lolley," she concluded.

She also believes Hutto was conveniently targeted as Lolley's murderer. In her opinion, Hutto was a suspect because he "ran around with Bradley" during their teenage and early adulthood years.

Another law enforcement officer, one who was heavily involved in trying to solve the murder case, remembered Bradley was immediately considered a prime suspect, but it was "hard to pin anything on him." However, Hutto was seen as the "weak link" who under pressure from the authorities might ultimately confess the name of the true killer.

Interestingly, Billy Wayne Bradley reappeared in Enterprise and was present during one or both of Hutto's 1977 murder trials. Two witnesses specifically remembered him sitting among the spectators in the crowded gallery. Bradley was obviously interested in hearing witness testimony and learning what the state had uncovered about Lolley's murder.

Karen Hudson Miller, a close friend of the Lolley family, was among those people waiting inside the courthouse for the jury to return with a verdict in the second trial. While there, she encountered Bradley for the first and only time in her life.

After her aunt acknowledged his presence, Bradley sneered at both women: "I didn't kill that old man."

For Karen, it proved to be a memorable introduction to a frightening man. Bradley's menacing manner and harsh tone left her with cold chills, and she rapidly exited the courtroom.

Unlike David Hutto, who is not known to have committed any crimes after his acquittal in the second murder trial, Billy Wayne Bradley's involvement in criminal acts continued throughout much of his life. A search of public records revealed Bradley was arrested and convicted for drug possession on three separate occasions (1980, 1984, and 2000) along with an unspecified felony third-degree conviction (2000). Bradley's final release from incarceration occurred on August 31, 2004, just over a year before his death at the age of 61.

An overwhelming majority of the people interviewed for this book who knew both Hutto and Bradley and provided crucial background information on both men opined Bradley was most likely Lolley's killer. More than 44 years after he unsuccessfully prosecuted David Hutto for the murder of Buford Lolley, former Assistant District Attorney Dale Marsh was open and frank when discussing this case.

"The thought among local law enforcement was that Billy Wayne Bradley did it," Marsh recalled.

The murder of Buford Lolley was certainly an act of rage. Rather that shooting the gas station attendant who likely could have identified the robbers, the murderer struck Lolley once on his arm and delivered at least seven savage blows to his skull, battering his head into a bloody pulp, even as the victim pled, "Help, help, help me."

Michael Lolley, Buford's nephew, one-time Enterprise chief of police, and a lifetime law enforcement officer, has investigated more than his share of murders. In his opinion, rageful homicide, which is substantiated by forensic psychiatric studies, is often associated with "the victim knowing the offender" or "the enjoyment of the event."

Buford Lolley knew both David Hutto and Billy Wayne Bradley. As far as deriving pleasure from brutally beating a man to death, Hutto, who was known to get queasy at the sight of blood, fails to match the profile of Lolley's killer.

There are many long-standing rumors about Buford Lolley's murder, many of which are unsubstantiated and not included in this book. However, four long-time Enterprise residents identified another potential suspect. His first name was also *David*. Hereafter, he will be referred to as David X, lacking any direct evidence to place him at or near the Save-Way on the morning of January 14, 1968.

One person remembered that David X "hung out" with Billy Wayne Bradley more often than David Hutto in the mid to late 1960s. This same individual recalled David X was "nutso and seeking attention." The second person described him as "crazy and mean as hell." A third local resident remembered David X "stayed in bad trouble all the time." The fourth person acknowledged the youth in question was a known member of Enterprise's so-called "wild crowd."

David X was afforded a layer of protection that was not available to David Hutto. His father was not only financially prosperous but also politically and socially well-connected in the community. The X family also lived in a much more affluent section of town than the Hutto clan did. Although no evidence was uncovered to reinforce this supposition, David X's father had enough money and influence to potentially shield his son from investigation in the Lolley murder case. Like Hutto and Bradley, David X is now deceased. The possibility that David Hutto was mistaken for David X, based solely on the latter's unsavory reputation, is just one example of the unanswered mysteries surrounding Buford Lolley's murder.

In conclusion, it is reasonable to postulate that David Hutto may well have participated in the robbery and witnessed someone else brutally murder Buford Lolley, but it appears highly unlikely he was a hardened sociopath or rageful enough to commit such a heinous act.

CHAPTER 12

In retrospect

F OR REASONS THAT ARE UNCLEAR, BUFORD Lolley's obituary was never
printed in *The Enterprise Ledger*. Mike Thompson, who began working at
Searcy Funeral Home in August of 1968, a bit over seven months after Lolley
was murdered, believes it is likely the mortuary performed the embalming
and cosmetic services after completing his autopsy. However, the funeral
home has no archived records for verification.

"In 1968, the newspaper would send a reporter to the funeral home to
write down the facts of the funeral by longhand. They would then take that
back to their office and do the organizing and typesetting. We did not have
the full obituary available to us. We only had the facts," Thompson later
recalled.

He did, however, uncover information about the murder victim's burial.
At 2:30 p.m., on Tuesday, January 16, 1968, Lolley's funeral services were
held at Shady Grove Baptist Church. Afterward, he was buried in the
cemetery adjacent to the church.

After reviewing the limited information available to him, Thompson
was most gracious in sharing what he discovered: "I hope you understand
the bookkeeping and recordkeeping during that time was not what it is now.
Also, the men that were working during that time have all passed away."

Lolley's sister-in-law, Mavis, recalled Buford's mother "grieved herself
to death" after her son's murder. Georgia Lee Lolley died on December
28, 1968, at Enterprise's Gibson Hospital, only 18 days shy of the one-year

anniversary of Buford's death. Unlike the case with her son, Mrs. Lolley's obituary was published in *The Enterprise Ledger*. She was buried next to her husband, John, and son, Buford, at Shady Grove Cemetery (also known as McCall Cemetery) in Samson, Alabama. Their final resting place is about 25 miles southwest of Enterprise.

Both residences where Buford was known to have spent his adult life are still standing. The family farm is on the southern edge of Enterprise at 4805 Boll Weevil Circle. The house where Lolley was living with his mother and sister at the time of his death, 730 Bellwood Road, is only 0.6 miles from where the Save-Way gas station once stood.

David Hutto, the man indicted, arrested, tried, and ultimately acquitted for the murder of Buford Lolley, died on February 11, 2016, at the age of 67. Hutto is buried adjacent to his mother and father at Meadowlawn Cemetery in Enterprise.

Hutto is survived by his wife, Susan. She was steadfastly loyal to her husband throughout his incarceration and murder trials, and at the time of David's death, the couple had been married for 45 years. David's two children, Kim Hutto Mitchell (and her husband Terry) and Chris Hutto, live just north of Enterprise on the same acreage as their mother. Hutto is also survived by three grandchildren, Tanna, Taryn, and Konnor. David did not live long enough to witness the birth of his first great-grandchild, Ryan.

The house David Hutto's mother was renting on Mill Street in January of 1968 was razed many years ago. An empty lot sits in its place, and the question as to whether the house was ever equipped with a chimney remains unanswered.

The Save-Way gas station, which was located at 716 South Main Street, remained in operation until 1980 when Leon Devane retired. The station continued 24-hour-a-day operations for another 10 years or so after Lolley's murder before Devane started closing at 6:00 p.m. each day.

Leon Devane's son, Vance, who was 12 years old when Buford Lolley was murdered, worked at the gas station as a teenager. In fact, much to his mother's chagrin, he sometimes manned the same graveyard shift as Buford Lolley. But there was one big difference: Vance always kept the pistol in his pocket rather than stored in the lockbox.

When Vance worked at Save-Way in the wee hours of the morning, an Enterprise police officer "would stop by every one to two hours to make sure

I was okay." On one occasion, he fell asleep in his chair during the winter months while the front door was locked and was awakened by "three or four policemen beating on the window to make sure I wasn't dead."

When Leon Devane retired, he sold the station's gas pumps to another Enterprise resident who owned and operated convenience stores. Those same pumps were relocated to one of those stores in another part of Enterprise. The former Save-Way building was razed sometime in the mid-1980s. Today, a muffler shop occupies the same spot where one of the most brutal murders in Enterprise history was committed.

Leon Devane, the savvy and hard-working owner of the Save-Way gas station, retired at age 59. He was tragically killed in a car accident on September 3, 2003.

Steve Weekley, the man who arrested David Hutto for murder, retired from the Alabama Bureau of Investigation in 1988. He resides in Enterprise.

Howard Murdock, the Enterprise chief of police at the time of Buford Lolley's murder and David Hutto's murder trials, died on January 26, 1980, at the age of 59. He is buried at Calvary Baptist Church Cemetery in Enterprise, next to his wife, Virginia, who died in 1987.

Terry Butts, who presided over both of Hutto's trials, served as a judge in Alabama's 12th Judicial Circuit for 18 years. Afterward, he was elected as a justice to the Alabama State Supreme Court. He later lost by a narrow margin in the general election to become Alabama's lieutenant governor. Today, Butts resides in Luverne, Alabama and maintains a private law practice.

Lewey L. Stephens, Jr. served for 18 years as the district attorney for the 12th Judicial Circuit. During his tenure as a prosecutor, Stephens tried more cases in more Alabama courthouses than any district attorney in the state's history. After formally retiring in 1978, he was designated as supernumerary district attorney throughout the state of Alabama and was awarded the moniker "Super D.A." Stephens died on July 4, 1982, at the age of 58. In 1991, the newly constructed district attorney's office building in Enterprise was named in honor of both Stephens and the legendary 12th district attorney and judge, Eris F. Paul.

After more than two years on the job, Assistant District Attorney Dale Marsh resigned and devoted his career to private practice. Heeding the advice of his mentor, Judge Eris Paul, who told him to "never enter politics," Marsh was not tempted to seek election as district attorney. Today, the location of his law office in Enterprise is a short walk from the auxiliary county courthouse.

David Hutto's senior defense attorney, Joe S. Pittman, was not only a skilled lawyer but also a talented businessman. Along with his two brothers, a physician and an engineer, the trio developed many residential and commercial properties in Enterprise. Joe Pittman died on October 16, 2006, at the age of 82.

After Dale Marsh resigned as assistant district attorney, David Hutto's other defense lawyer, Ken Hooks, took over the position and served under two district attorneys, Lewey L. Stephens, Jr. and Joel Folmar. For 10 years, Hooks was married to Joe Pitman's daughter, Pam, before the couple divorced. In 1981, Hooks moved to Birmingham, Alabama to join Lanny Vines and Associates, one of the most successful plaintiff's law firms in the country. Eventually, he formed his own practice, Ken Hooks Law, a firm specializing in civil litigation. Today, Hooks is semi-retired and still lives in Birmingham.

Enterprise's decrepit white brick auxiliary county courthouse, constructed in 1925 and the site of David Hutto's 1977 murder trials, was razed in 1998. A much larger and more modern building was constructed on the same site as its predecessor, 99 Edwards Street. The new county courthouse was formally dedicated in 1999.

Since 1968, much has changed in Enterprise, Alabama. The population has nearly doubled, and with so many businesses located on the traffic circle, downtown is no longer the unrivaled center of action. Many of the buildings that once graced Main Street have been renovated or simply torn down. Some of the structures look much the same but are unoccupied. Except for the churches, hardly any structure on the town's main thoroughfare bears the same name as it did over a half-century ago.

Through the efforts of entrepreneurs, new business owners, and concerned citizens, all dedicated to maintaining a viable downtown area, the very heart of Enterprise is certainly different than it appeared in the past, yet the town remains very much alive. The former Seaboard Coastline Railroad depot building, now known as the Enterprise Depot Museum, and the Rawls Hotel have joined the Boll Weevil Monument on the National Historic Register. The only statue in the world glorifying an agricultural pest continues to stand proud in the middle of Main Street, maintaining a watchful eye over its surroundings.

The horrifying murder of Buford Lolley in 1968 forever scarred his family. While he may be gone, he is not forgotten.

In late December of 1976, suddenly and without warning, David Hutto was arrested for murder. Even though he was eventually acquitted, the stigma can never be fully erased, though he and his family endured the distasteful memory with dignity and courage.

For the Lolley and Hutto families, the past cannot be changed. Hopefully, their misfortunes will benefit from reexamination under an objective light.

Even though partial closure to this chain of ugly events may have been realized, those who recall the brutal murder that occurred on January 14, 1968, will never forget the day when evil visited Enterprise, Alabama.

EPILOGUE

The missing files

I BEGAN PREPARING TO WRITE THIS BOOK in early May of 2021 by outlining the structure, formulating an extensive list of personal interviews, and attempting to compile the research materials needed to complete the task. I began the first formal interviews later that same month.

The opportunity to peruse official records is crucial when writing non-fiction. In my 15 previous non-fiction books, I have benefitted greatly from legal and unhampered access to such materials. This book, unfortunately, has proved to be the lone exception.

I want to make it clear that I admire and respect law enforcement officers. In my office, I proudly display a South Carolina State Trooper's patch that was generously given to me. I began this book with hopes that local and state law enforcement agencies would be valuable research tools. Perhaps naively so, I thought investigators might welcome a public reexamination of this cold case murder. In addition, I was of the opinion law enforcement standards for maintaining records, particularly those related to unsolved cases, would equal or exceed what is mandated for physicians.

The district attorney's office in Alabama's 12th Judicial Circuit was most cooperative. But through no fault of their own, the trial transcripts from 1977 were apparently destroyed, which is not uncommon after a defendant is acquitted, eliminating the need for subsequent judicial appeals.

My experiences with local and state law enforcement agencies, however, were quite the opposite. After sending two emails to the Enterprise Police Department (EPD) in late May or early June, both of which were unanswered, a local and influential intermediary contacted the police chief. Soon afterward, I received a return email from the police chief apologizing for the delayed response. At that time, I was informed the EPD would search for the Lolley cold-case murder file and hopefully have it available for my examination when I arrived in Enterprise in early July for my hands-on research.

As the time neared for my trip to Enterprise, I again emailed the chief of police. In his return email, the chief informed me the file had not been located. But he assured me that if it was found after my trip to the Enterprise, the EPD would mail me a copy. I have since learned any such action would likely have been a violation of Alabama statute Title 12-21-3.1.

The Lolley cold case file was accessible by members of the EPD as recently as 1995, according to a former police officer who examined its contents. As the summer of 2021 passed, I waited patiently, hoping the file would eventually be found. During that time, to ensure that I had done everything possible to gain access to available files, I sent Freedom of Information Act (FOIA) requests to not only the Enterprise Police Department but also the Alabama Bureau of Investigation and the Cold Case Division of the Alabama State Attorney General's Office.

Nearing the end of August, I communicated with Enterprise's city attorney about my desire to access the Lolley file. He reported that the EPD still had not located the file.

On September 1, I emailed the chief of police of Enterprise: "I have not checked in (with you) for several weeks. I was hoping you might have had some success in locating the file."

The tone of the police chief's return email was unexpected: "We are still engaged in looking for the Lolley file, and if/when we locate it, you will be the first to know. However, understand current operations within the police department take precedence over cases from 50 years ago. I will do what I can and so will CID, but we cannot dedicate manpower to strictly searching for this file while we have current investigations to attend to."

Somewhat taken aback by the chief's email, I answered him the following day: "I fear that I may have offended you with my repeat emails and FOIA request. Please know that I have never expected anyone in the Enterprise Police Department to prioritize looking for a more than half-century-old cold case file over current and more important law enforcement responsibilities. Since the trial transcripts from 1977 were not retained, the EPD and ABI are my only hopes for any official documentation as I come close to completing this book. I am certain both files could plug holes in the storyline, and I owe it to myself and my readers to explore every source thoroughly."

I never received a return email from the police chief. And at the time of publication, the EPD has yet to notify me about whether the cold-case murder file has been located.

My experiences with law enforcement at the state level were also less than satisfactory. Even though the Alabama attorney general's office has a dedicated cold case division, no one from that office bothered to acknowledge my FOIA request, much less offer any assistance or encouragement. In fact, none of the three agencies who were recipients of my FOIA requests ever acknowledged receiving my formal inquiries.

On June 24, 2021, I sent a lengthy email to the designated address on the Alabama Bureau of Investigation's web page (sbi.investigations@alea.gov). In that email, I requested access to any files related to the 1968 cold case murder of Buford Lolley, while also explaining the scope of my book project and offering a brief author biography. Three days later, having received no acknowledgment of my first email, I sent an identical message. There was still no reply. A few days later, I sent yet a third email request. No official from the ABI acknowledged any of the three emails. By this time, I was uncertain how to establish contact with the ABI.

On July 2nd, a law enforcement agent in the Enterprise area agreed to contact a friend and former colleague who is currently employed as an agent with the ABI. That same day, when the ABI agent called me, I informed him about the book I was writing as well as my earlier unsuccessful attempts to communicate with the ABI. For the next three weeks, I exchanged emails and phone calls with him concerning the file search. The agent informed me several times that he had spoken with a supervisor who indicated an active search was being undertaken for any files related to the Lolley cold-case murder. The agent also secured a letter from one of Buford Lolley's next of kin, which was supposedly necessary to authorize the release of this file. At the request of his unnamed supervisor, I provided him with the name of my website, offering proof I was a legitimate author. I also informed him I had submitted a FOIA request to the ABI officially asking for access to all files related to the murder of Buford Lolley and the arrest of David Hutto. I continued to communicate with the investigator through August 23rd, during which time he expressed hope and enthusiasm that the file would eventually be recovered. The ABI investigator was always pleasant and encouraging, never once indicated he was bothered by my weekly text messages or phone calls.

After August 23rd, suddenly and without forewarning, the ABI investigator stopped responding to my text messages or answering my phone calls. At this point, I still had no idea about the status of my request to examine the cold-case file and could only assume the agent had been ordered to cease communication with me or had done so of his own volition. Having now lost my sole ABI contact, I was uncertain of how to proceed. While prior attempts to contact anyone in a leadership position in state law enforcement via email had been unsuccessful, I decided to once again pursue this method of inquiry.

Consequently, on September 7th, I sent a fourth email to the Criminal Investigation Division of the ABI: "If you check your email files, I have sent three separate emails about the cold case murder files on Buford E. Lolley, who was killed on 1-14-1968 in Enterprise, Alabama, and the arrest of a suspect, David Hutto, by former ABI investigator Steve Weekley on 12-13-1976. The suspect, David Hutto, was tried twice—one ended in a mistrial and the second in an acquittal. I am seeking to access those files as part of (my) research for a forthcoming book about this murder. To date, no one from ABI has even acknowledged receiving my emails. My attorney wants to know if a gag order has been issued. As a starting point, can I at least receive acknowledgment of this email?"

The following morning, I received an email from the chief of the Criminal Investigation Division. Finally, after more than two months, this represented my first communication from a ranking ABI official.

The chief's reply was short and to the point: "I am in receipt of your email, dated 9-7-21 at 4:44 p.m., regarding your request of case files pertaining to Buford E. Lolley. In accordance with the Code of Alabama, Title 12-21-3.1, the State Bureau of Investigation does not release case files upon public request."

Suddenly but belatedly, the realization hit me that I was never going to be granted access to the Lolley cold-case files. This unexpected revelation left several unanswered questions. Why did it take more than two months to inform me of this fact? Would I have *ever* been informed about the statute forbidding disclosure of case files to public inquires had I not sent a fourth email? Had the ABI not received prior requests to examine criminal case files from authors and journalists? Were there any exceptions to the statue allowing examination of redacted documents, even if it necessitated my traveling to Montgomery and reviewing the materials under close supervision? Why had my earlier source not been made aware of the prohibitory statue prior to offering me assistance? (For the first time, I mentioned the agent by name, even though his communication with me had unexplainably ended some two weeks earlier.)

That same day, I emailed the chief of the Criminal Investigation Division, sharing my confusion and posing those same questions to him. I also indicated I would be willing to travel from South Carolina to Alabama to examine any available files and allowable information related to this murder.

I concluded this same email, pointing out that writers must be true to themselves and straightforward with their readers: "If your decision is final, I will have to explain my lengthy, non-communicative journey with the ABI as well as being misled by the ABI in my book, not out of frustration, but to explain to my readers why no official documents were made available. But I will have to tell the entire story of being both misled and ignored."

When the chief failed to answer this message, I emailed him again that same day and asked if he would, at the very least, answer my questions. He again did not answer my email. Later that same day, I received a telephone call from ABI's general counsel.

The attorney was most courteous and generous with his time. He fully explained statute 12-21-3.1, prohibiting any examination of the cold case murder files, absent filing a lawsuit for disclosure. I assured him I did not have the inclination, time, or financial resources to pursue litigation. I did point out if I had been informed about the statute when I first contacted the ABI over two months ago, I would not have persisted in my efforts to obtain those files. Since I had been inadvertently misled about the possibility of obtaining the file by a friendly and well-meaning agent, I found it both strange and frustrating that no one in a leadership position at the ABI took time to correct this misconception until I pushed the envelope. I also explained to the attorney my obligation to document this futile and byzantine journey with the ABI in my book. I was further surprised to learn that the general counsel had not been advised of my earlier FOIA request.

I exchanged several phone calls with ABI's general counsel over the coming days. After our initial conversation, he personally undertook a search for the cold-case murder file, including a perusal of records stored at the Alabama State Archives. At this point in time, no one could *locate* the cold case file. I shared my shock and amazement with the attorney that the two law enforcement agencies responsible for the investigation of Buford Lolley's murder were unable to produce *any* documentation. I also made it a point to inform him that my book would not reveal the names of local or state law enforcement officials who had communicated with me during the unsuccessful file search. Despite poor communication, misleading information, and the inability to locate files, which I consider to be inexcusable, it is not my intention to embarrass anyone. In the unlikely event new evidence were to emerge in Buford Lolley's murder case, how would the Enterprise Police Department and the Alabama Bureau of Investigation handle the situation? How embarrassing would it be to explain to another law enforcement agency that the original files were lost or misfiled?

I am certain this book would be more comprehensive had I been granted access to the cold-case files at both the state and local levels. Even if the EPD and ABI eventually locate the missing files, it is frustrating to me as a writer and a native Alabamian, particularly in a state where the attorney general's office features a dedicated cold-case murder division, that there is such a state of disorder involving the storage of reports related to unsolved homicides. While I understand the nature of bureaucracies, it is unfortunate that a law enforcement agency refused to communicate with me for more than eight weeks after three inquiries. In the end, I received no reliable information until I was forced to push harder.

After extensively researching this case, I have no reason to believe either the local or state law enforcement agencies have attempted to disclose any improprieties associated with this murder investigation. At the same time, I will not be surprised if some readers find it suspicious that the two law enforcement agencies responsible for investigating this murder cannot locate their files. And if the files are eventually found, this same segment of the readership may distrust their content.

Lacking any desire to pen an exposé, I regrettably considered it necessary to fully explain my inability to access official files related to this case in the epilogue.

AFTERWORD

RESEARCHING AND WRITING A BOOK ABOUT events that transpired in my hometown has been a rewarding experiencing. I was privileged to communicate with a number of interesting people, many of whom I had never met before. An overwhelming majority of those individuals were generous with their time, memories, and insights. I am grateful for the opportunity to renew old acquaintances and make new friends. Wherever I reside, Enterprise, Alabama will always be home.

Revisiting this murder occasionally unleashed a wave of distasteful emotions, including horror, disgust, frustration, and anger. At the same time, the look back was a pleasant reminder of simpler times. Exploring distant tragedy and injustice, while not always uplifting, was a journey well spent.

This book was not written with the unrealistic goal of solving a cold case murder committed over a half-century ago. Hopefully, it has shed a neglected light on past events and enabled readers to formulate their own theories about who likely ended the life of an innocent man.

Buford Lolley deserves to be remembered as much more than the name of a murder victim printed in black ink on the pages of yellowing newspapers. He was a living, breathing human being who was loved and respected. The tragedy that befell him was not of his own making. He was a good and decent man who unfortunately found himself at the wrong place at the wrong time.

And time can never be reversed for the Hutto family. However, if David Hutto can be regarded as a likely scapegoat rather than an accused killer, perhaps his family and closest friends can find some measure of solace.

May Buford Lolley rest in peace with the acknowledgment that he has not been forgotten, and may the Hutto family remember the good times they enjoyed with David, a man they lovingly knew as a husband, father, and grandfather.

Source Notes

Face-to-face interviews, telephone interviews, and/ or email exchanges:

Mavis Lolley (sister-in-law of Buford Lolley)

Michael Lolley (long-time law enforcement officer and nephew of Buford Lolley)

Karen Hudson Miller (volunteer at the Pea River Historical Society and close friend of the Lolley family)

Susan Hutto (wife of David Hutto)

Kim Hutto Mitchell (daughter of David Hutto)

Chris Hutto (son of David Hutto)

Terry Mitchell (son-in-law of David Hutto)

Taryn Outlaw (granddaughter of David Hutto)

Ray Milligan (long-time friend of David Hutto)

Steve Weekley (ABI Investigator who arrested David Hutto for murder)

Terry Butts (presiding circuit judge in both of David Hutto's murder trials)

Dale Marsh (assistant district attorney during both of David Hutto's murder trials)

Ken Hooks (one of David Hutto's two defense attorneys)

Jim Ellis (circuit court clerk during both of David Hutto's trials)

Don Pittman (Enterprise attorney and nephew of the late Joe Pittman)

Gary McAliley (retired circuit court judge and district attorney)

Crys Fuller (administrative assistant at the 12th Judicial Circuit district attorney's office)

Daniel Stephens (son of former District Attorney Lewey L. Stephens, Jr.)

Larry Baxter (former Enterprise Police Department officer)

Vance Devane (retired health care comptroller/CFO and the son of Save-Way gas station owner, Leon Devane)

Ricky Adams (journalist, columnist, and noted Enterprise historian)

Eddie Lammon (retired veterinarian and contemporary of David Hutto, Billy Wayne Bradley, David X, and others)

John McCrummen (financial services manager, pastor, and David Hutto's friend)

Billie Patrick (Long-time Enterprise resident and childhood neighbor of Billy Wayne Bradley)

Mike Thompson (long-time employee of Searcy Funeral Home)

Tonya Michelle Howell (daughter of Ned Howell)

Interview and contact facilitators:

Mark Fuller (attorney, former judge, and Enterprise native, who lives in Montgomery, Alabama)

Jim Reese (retired educator and school superintendent, author, and long-time Enterprise native)

Herbert Gannon, Jr. (retired physician and Enterprise native, who lives in Birmingham, Alabama)

Tim Whitehead (retired businessman and long-time Enterprise resident)

Pam McQueen (Long-time Enterprise resident, who is quite well-versed on local history)

Onsite Resources

The Pea River Historical and Genealogical Society

The Enterprise Depot Museum

Newspaper articles

The Enterprise Ledger

The Daily Ledger

The Elba News

The Dothan Eagle

The Montgomery Advertiser

Books and reference articles

Reese, Jim. *This Ain't No Shoe Store*! 2nd Edition. Amazon Publishing, 2020.

Shoffner, Roy. *Dateline Enterprise*. Rose Printing Company, 1987.

Annals of the Entomological Society of America

Internet resources

peoplelegacy.com
findagrave.com
newspapers.com
alpeanuts.com
census.com
cityofenterprise.net
srh.noaa
eprisenow.com
enterpriselibrary.org
enterpriseschools.net
peariver.org
bioguide.congress.gov
truthfinder.com
coffeecounty.us
projectcoldcase.org
thedisastercenter.com
archives.gov
searcyfuneralhome.com
encyclopediaofalabama.org
enterpriseal.gov
citytourinfo.com
tuskegee.edu
roadsideamerica.com
townsquarepublications.com

ACKNOWLEDGEMENTS

I OWE AN IMMEASURABLE DEBT OF GRATITUDE to the people who willingly and most often enthusiastically allowed me to interview them about this cold-case murder. Many of those same individuals, after initial lengthy interviews, kindly answered follow-up questions via emails, text messages, and phone calls. If I inadvertently missed listing any of the interviewees, I profoundly apologize. For those who did not want their names to appear in the source notes, I respected your wishes while remaining grateful for your assistance. In addition, I appreciate the facilitators who not only helped me track down various people who remember this case but also kindly vouched for my personal and professional credibility.

I appreciate Dieon Patton contributing a photograph of the 1970s-era auxiliary Coffee County Courthouse in Enterprise, featured on the cover of this book. Patton's many photographs of Enterprise and the surrounding area are true works of art.

Two people deserve special thanks. Kim Hutto Mitchell and Karen Hudson Miller took time away from their otherwise busy schedules to assist me in multiple different ways, while I spent the vast majority of my time researching and writing this book some 400 miles distant from Enterprise. I thank both of you from the bottom of my heart.

I appreciate the many contributions of Dale Marsh, who was the assistant district attorney during both of David Hutto's murder trials. Without hesitation, Dale helped me better understand many details associated with this case. I thank you for your time and excellent memory.

Sharon James, my talented editor, made my words more readable. Thank you, Sharon.

My wife, Anne, consistently supports me when I am intently focused on the writing project at hand. She patiently and lovingly endures life with a practicing physician and a part-time writer. She has also proven to be a valuable assistant during book-related research trips. I love you very much.

My sons, Andy and Ben, and my daughter-in-law, Abbey, are the lights of my life. I love you more than I can put into words.

To the readers, I once again thank you for your continued support of my "Bringing History Alive" series. I hope you found *A Lingering Evil: The Unsolved Murder of Buford Lolley* interesting and informative. For fellow natives of Lower Alabama, I hope this book brought back distant memories of people, places, and events, not all of which were unpleasant.

ABOUT THE AUTHOR

Jeffrey K. Smith is a physician and a writer. A native of Enterprise, Alabama, he earned his undergraduate and medical degrees from the University of Alabama. After completing his residency at the William S. Hall Psychiatric Institute, Dr. Smith entered private practice in Upstate South Carolina. The author and his wife, Anne, reside in Greer, South Carolina. They are the proud parents of two sons, Andy and Ben.

Dr. Smith is the author of three murder-mystery novels and 16 works of non-fiction, the latter representing his "Bringing History Alive" series. To learn more the author's books, please visit www.newfrontierpublications.net.

OTHER BOOKS BY JEFFREY K. SMITH

Fiction

Sudden Despair
Two Down, Two to Go
A Phantom Killer

Non-fiction

Rendezvous in Dallas: The Assassination of John F. Kennedy (two editions)

The Fighting Little Judge: The Life and Times of George C. Wallace

Fire in the Sky: The Story of the Atomic Bomb

Bad Blood: Lyndon B. Johnson, Robert F. Kennedy,
and the Tumultuous 1960s (two editions)

Dixiecrat: The Life and Times of Strom Thurmond

The Loyalist: The Life and Times of Andrew Johnson

The Eagle Has Landed: The Story of Apollo 11

The Presidential Assassins: John Wilkes Booth, Charles Julius
Guiteau, Leon Frank Czolgosz, and Lee Harvey Oswald

Jeffrey K. Smith

The War on Crime: J. Edgar Hoover Versus the John Dillinger Gang

The Wizard of the Saddle: General Nathan Bedford Forrest

*You Were Right and We Were Wrong: The Life and
Times of Judge Frank M. Johnson, Jr.*

Grover Cleveland: The Last Conservative Democratic President

Listen To Me: The Brief Life and Enduring Legacy of Buddy Holly

A Family Affair: The Rosenberg Espionage Case

A Prelude to War: The Presidency of James Buchanan

The Assistant President: South Carolina's James F. Byrnes

CPSIA information can be obtained
at www.ICGtesting.com
Printed in the USA
LVHW091456250222
711901LV00007B/251